After the Rain

A Novel of War and Coming Home

John M. Archer

Dec 7, 2019
Gettysburg, PA

For Joseph —
I hope you enjoy Spenser's
Journey —

PUBLISHED BY MAURYBOOKS

Printed and Bound in the United States of America

ISBN: 978-0-9963455-3-8

Cover Image: Pursuit of Lee's Army. Marching Through the Rain," Original oil on canvas by Edwin Forbes. Image courtesy Library of Congress

Cover design by author

Dedicated to all
Whose hearts were touched with fire

We saw the lightning and that was the guns;

And then we heard the thunder and that was the big guns;

And then we heard the rain falling and that was the blood falling;

And when we came to get in the crops,

It was dead men that we reaped.

- Harriet Tubman, United States

And the blood of brave men was shed like unto the shedding of rain from a black cloud.

- Ferdowsi Tousi, Persia

Tomorrow maybe love, but now it is the rain

Possesses us entirely, the twilight and the rain.

- Alun Lewis, Wales

PREFACE

With the passing of one-hundred and fifty years, the nightmare that was the American Civil War is still at the heart of the United States and its people. Over that time, countless works of fact and fiction have attempted to define this crucible of our history; not surprisingly, most focus on the larger picture: famous leaders, great battles, and colorful characters. In this view, the millions of average soldiers who bore the brunt of the war's carnage form only a backdrop. Doubtless, glimpses of their wartime experiences appear in published letters and diaries, but with the return of the veterans to hearth and home after the war, their lives – and their reactions to the horrors of the killing fields – fall again from our view.

The suggestion that grim memories haunted their homecomings might seem melodramatic: the popular image of the veterans of the Blue and the Gray is one of friendly handshakes at blameless reunions. Were the motivations behind that war's bloodshed somehow more noble, sparing the veterans unsettling memories of the battlefield? Considering the state of medicine in the 1800's, and the inconsistent record keeping following the war, the notion might not be surprising. However, nineteenth-century physicians did note odd, and often severe, emotional and physical reactions from exposure to combat; termed "*nostalgia*" or "*soldier's heart*" at the time, these ailments today sound almost benign.

Over time, doctors tried to better define the trauma, coining now-familiar terms for the symptoms: World War I veterans had *shell shock*, those who suffered in World War II and Korea had *battle fatigue*; today these same symptoms are described as *post-traumatic stress disorder*. Regardless of the time period, or the words used to describe the suffering, these terms do little to describe the ordeal endured by these veterans and their families long after the guns went silent.

This tale hopes to say more.

I expected to be happy [at home} and I was for a little while, but it is not so now, my heart has wedge thrown upon it which cannot be easily taken off. It pains me. I may forget it a minute or two, but it will come in my mind again; I try all in the world to be happy and others that see me think so, but there is something that works in me I dare not to explain...

– Lt. Charles Leuschner, 6th Texas Infantry, June 15, 1865 diary entry

As long as reason holds her sway, until all else is forgotten, I shall remember that day and its ghastly dead.

- Pvt. Sherman Norris, 7th Ohio Infantry, 1888 Reunion

I cannot comment more, nor dwell on the subject. I am so unwell.

- Capt. Stephen Lowing, 3rd Michigan Infantry, Letter to sister

PART I
WAR

In Eighteen–hundred and sixty–two, America's Civil War was in its second year. In his first months of command, Confederate General Robert E. Lee had achieved remarkable success in Virginia against a substantially larger Federal Army. On the heels of his victory at the Second Battle of Bull Run, Lee led his men into the border state of Maryland. Another victory against the Union Army, this time north of the Potomac, would threaten Baltimore or Washington, and the North would have no choice but to acknowledge the South's independence. His plans quickly went awry; before Lee could concentrate his force in Maryland, the Union Army under Major General George McClellan threatened to crush the invaders in detail. To salvage the invasion, Lee ordered his forces to reunite outside of Sharpsburg. Confidently pursuing the Rebels, McClellan found the Southern army with their back to the Potomac River – no longer retreating, but offering battle on rolling high ground above Antietam Creek.

September 16, 1862: Evening
North of Sharpsburg, Maryland

The landscape of western Maryland above the Potomac River is a bit odd: thick ledges of gray-black rock cut the fertile hollows of ochre soil; ribbed snake rail fences and bone-hued limestone walls hem the tidy farmsteads; twisted scrub vies with tall, broad-leaved trees for space and sun in the woodlots; picturesque perhaps, but also a fitting backdrop for a nightmare.

The old Smoketown Road – really not much more than a farm lane – is one of the narrow ways that wind through this terrain east of the Potomac; it in turn, connects to an equally narrow path bridging the tributary known as Antietam Creek. Sunset that September evening found the road choked with thousands of Federal soldiers; caked in dust, sweat-soaked blue uniforms packed the twisting lane for three miles back over the stone bridge that spanned the creek. The snail-like fits and starts pace of the march, the stifling air, and choking dust frayed at a man's nerves; any sudden halt collapsed the column like a train wreck, the rear ranks pushing into those in front amid a stream of curses. But the burst of gunfire that echoed from the woods ahead was ample reason to stop. Muttered complaints still ran down the lane. *Some jumpy fools just got ambushed by a pig...* The deeper thump of artillery rolled over the crack of rifle fire, and the grumbling stopped. *No. That's Rebs...*

Near the back of the column, the lieutenant winced and set his jaw. *And so it starts...* Spencer climbed up the earthen bank beside the lane to get a look at what was happening. Smoke hung in the humid air above the trees to the southwest, the gunfire rose and fell, but he could make out little else. *Someone is sure catching hell...* He drew in a slow breath through clenched teeth, and returned to the ranks to wait in the close air.

On the books, this was the 107th Pennsylvania Volunteer Regiment, just one small piece of McClellan's enormous Army of the Potomac. That

March, the regiment had marched proudly from Harrisburg with a thousand recruits; now, six months later, disease and Rebel lead had pared their number to fewer than two hundred. War's grim reckoning took a toll on officers as well: over the lieutenant's shoulder, Captain James MacThompson rode beside the column, commanding the regiment in the place of a colonel. Likewise, Daniel Spencer now led Company "B," a lieutenant serving in a captain's stead. That was the way of it. Spencer pulled off his cap, ran his fingers back through the matted hair, and closed his eyes. *And if I'm not up to it, I'll get us all killed...*

The bright foliage fell to shades of gray and black as they waited in the lane. Mounted couriers raced back and forth on either side of the column, while rumors of an innumerable Rebel foe ahead spread through the ranks. Then, almost as quickly as it started, the gunfire faded in the twilight. A rider stopped and spoke with Captain MacThompson. Hushed orders passed down the line: break ranks in silence and go into camp beside the road. Spencer turned and said quietly, "Company 'B' with me," and the group of twenty-odd filed off into a small, rocky pasture and stacked their rifles. Captain MacThompson made his way along the lane and rode up to Spencer.

"Lieutenant, the Rebs are just beyond those woods. General McClellan wants it quiet, and no fires for any reason." MacThompson then turned and rode off.

Spencer waved the company together; several of the men had already gathered an armload of branches and looked blankly at the lieutenant.

"Sorry boys, no fires. Cold supper tonight. Bed down and keep it quiet. The General doesn't want to give away our position."

"L'tenit? I 'spect the Rebs know we're here..." There was quiet laughter; Spencer smiled and held a finger to his lips. *Well, at least they're laughing.*

"Well soldier, you've got me there."

"No L'tenit, you got us here..."

More stifled laughs. The lieutenant frowned in the direction of the speaker; he waved off the gathering, turned and headed to the thin line of trees bordering the pasture. Spencer felt uneasy dismissing this camaraderie; he had known some of these men since childhood, and had befriended many more. But he was in command now. *A friend won't send you to die. They need a leader...* By the time he started pulling off his pack and haversack, his teeth had clenched again. *And if I'm not up to it, I'll get them all killed...* Spencer shook off the thought and reassured himself. *You can make a difference. You can lead...*

A slow drizzle began pattering the trees and he walked under the cover of a small oak to attempt some rest. Sanitation being what it was with armies on the move, before he sat down, the lieutenant inspected the ground in the dim light. On the other side of the tree, someone cleared their throat.

"Nobody's been here L'tenit. You can set down."

Spencer braced himself and peered around the tree in the gloom: Sergeant Quinn.

"Quinn! Dammit, you scared the hell out of me!"

The sergeant cackled, and turned toward him. "Just as well, L'tenit. Come morning, there'll be plenty of *hell* to go around."

Spencer wrapped his rubber blanket around his shoulders, settled into a spot at the base of the tree, and leaned back. *Plenty of hell to go around...* Quinn certainly had that right. Only three days before, it seemed the Rebel army was in retreat back to Virginia. Then the Southerners suddenly stopped and turned. The lieutenant shook his head. *With his back to the damn river, Lee throws down the gauntlet and stares. And McClellan just blinked. Then he wonders on how to surprise Lee. The sun has gone down twice since then, and this surprise attack just went into camp for the night. Hell, McClellan doesn't know what to do...* He winced. *Bobby Lee will certainly know what to do. He'll reinforce this end of the line, and come morning, the Rebs will give us hell.*

Spencer shook his head again and pulled the blanket tighter around his shoulders. He could picture Quinn sitting on the other side of the tree, motionless, drawing silently on his pipe. The sergeant had been a constant at his side in the days since Second Bull Run; there a chunk of Rebel iron tore into Captain John Dick and command of the company fell to Spencer, an inexperienced lieutenant. Quinn was of indeterminate age. Spencer thought him to be mid-forties or so, maybe older; no matter, he couldn't imagine what the younger version of the man might be like. It was clear Conall Quinn had seen much of warfare long before he ended up in this regiment. Spencer didn't know from what deep well the man drew his intuition of people and the way of it all, but he rarely questioned it; Quinn's advice was invaluable – and blunt. The lieutenant tried to frame his unease with words.

"Sergeant…"

"Yassir?" Quinn peered around the tree at him.

"A question for you Sergeant: you've been in the army since the beginning of this madness. What do you think about when you lead men…into battle?"

"You mean mebbe to *die*, don't you L'tenit? Wellsir. You can't think about that. Lord knows, we're all going to go sometime. Nowsir. I'd just as soon not be the cause of these men dyin'. They trust us. We need to trust ourselves that when the time comes, we'll do the right thing by 'em. L'tenit, you've only been in command two weeks. You've done fine – the boys respect you."

"But I don't see an end to this war – not soon anyway. You Conall, you just keep pushing. How do you keep on?"

"Wellsir. War? Everyone has his take on it, a'course. Mine says it's like climbing a mountain, it is. The job is to keep climbing until you get to the top: you know where you've been, so there's no point lookin' down. You leave that behind. Nowsir. There's some that fall in the climb that shouldn't; you know well enough about them. And there's some who get too used up to go on – get stuck, if you take my meaning. All they can do is hang there on the side of the damn mountain, lookin' back at where they been. Can't fight a lick. But L'tenit? Every mother's son will get too used up some day; the rub is making it to the top of the mountain before then. Nobody wins, sir. They just survive."

Spencer clenched his teeth and shivered in the dark. *Nobody wins… They just survive.* The Sergeant leaned around the tree: a whiskered, craggy face lit only by the glow of the pipe's embers. He looked at the lieutenant a moment, then said quietly, "Now, sir. Nothin' says I'm right about all this.

You asked…and you know how I do love to talk." Quinn cackled again and settled back into his spot.

Conall Quinn, you are more right than you know… Spencer huffed a sigh, leaned around the tree and looked at Quinn. "Well. Always obliged for your take, Sergeant. Better get some shuteye. If you're right, tomorrow is going to be one of those climbs you talked about."

Spencer sat back against the oak, rubbed his face and tried to relax. He thought of home. *Sarah…blue eyes in the dawn.* Their farm on the mountain was not all that far away – by a crow's flight, maybe thirty miles. His last furlough was only a month or so back; it might as well have been another lifetime. Quinn's words still hung in his ears. *Every mother's son will get too used up some day…*

Nearby, a low hum of whispers came from small, cheerless clusters of men. Without hearing clearly, Spencer understood the murmur: tomorrow would bring battle – maybe *the* battle – and many here will not make it through. *Hell of a way for a man to spend his last night: wet, cold, and hungry…* About midnight, the quiet rain turned to a steady downpour.

In the months following Antietam, General Lee scored several decisive, but fruitless victories on the now ravaged soil of Virginia. In the summer of 1863, Lee decided to invade the very heart of the North: Pennsylvania. There he hoped to gain badly needed supplies, but more importantly, score that decisive victory he was certain was still possible. On the first three days of July, Lee's seemingly invincible army went into battle at the crossroads town of Gettysburg. After three days of carnage, the Union Army had stalemated the Southern veterans. Lee turned his battered army back through the passes of the Catoctin Mountains and the safety of Virginia. Toiling in the midst of heavy rains, the wagon train bearing Lee's wounded was said to stretch for seventeen miles.

July 4, 1863: Afternoon
South Mountain, Pennsylvania

Almost invisible in the downpour, he splashed across the puddled yard and ran up the wide porch steps to the doorway beyond. Closing the door on the storm outside, Daniel turned to look about the silent room. He reassured himself one more time nothing had changed, but the feeling lingered. *No. Something feels different...* Unconsciously, he gave his soaked mackintosh two wet shrugs, pulled it off, and looped the collar over the peg beside the door. With more difficulty, he pulled off his sodden boots and dropped them by the threshold. He walked to the side window, gazing back out into the storm.

The rain. *The rain changes everything...* A downpour like this blurs the senses: sights and smells almost disappear. *The world renews...* Daniel ran his finger down the condensation at the edge of the pane, and a drop formed that ran slowly to the sill. *That's not it... None of this feels right.*

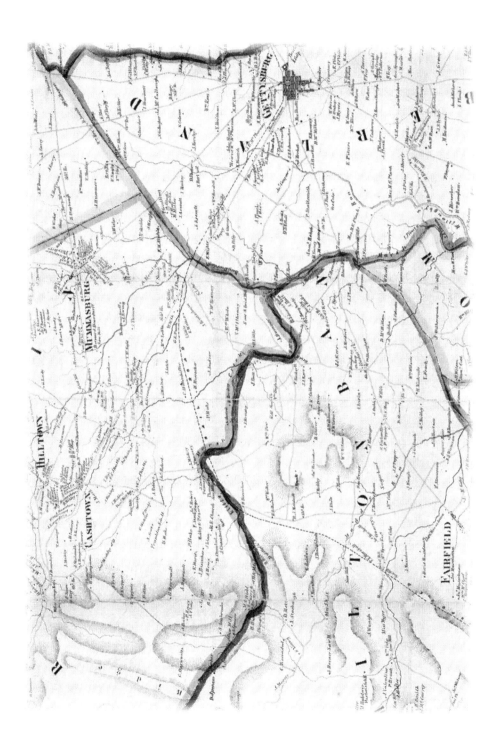

The Spencer farm sat high in one of the many folds of ground that cut into the northern arm of the Blue Ridge known as South Mountain. On a clear day, a sweeping view lay from the front porch across the low ridges below, and on to the county seat at Gettysburg ten miles away. This afternoon found most of the view lost in a wet haze. *Things sure as hell have changed down there...* The sounds of a battle from the town had rumbled up the mountainside since Wednesday; on Friday afternoon, the cannon had raged for two hours: he remembered all too well the paralyzing horror under those big guns. *Powerless...*

An uncanny silence now hushed up the mountainside; the struggle had come to a head. He took his tarnished field glass off the sill and once again scanned the rain-choked valley. Appearing out of the murk below, the gray-brown slash that marked the path of the Chambersburg Pike climbed the mountain north of the farm. There, the breaks in the haze confirmed his suspicions; the very road seemed to be moving: barely discernible in the gloom, a line of pale-hued wagons snaked toward the pass. "I'll be damned," he said to himself, "Lee is retreating…"

Only the week before, Daniel had watched an odd mixture of vehicles drawn by mules, horses, and oxen climbing the same road to make their way back to Virginia, groaning under the weight of supplies garnered by the Confederates in Pennsylvania. Now, a seemingly endless procession rolled over the Pike, groaning instead with the carnage of war. Whatever had happened at Gettysburg, the once proud army of Robert E. Lee was in retreat; rainwater washed the cost of that pride out of the wagons, and a red-tinged stream ran back down the road into the valley. "Rebel bastards," he muttered, "what made you believe this war was a good idea?"

Staring off into the mist, he could picture their long gray ranks charging from a cloud of dingy smoke. His ears rang again with the black roar of battle, rolling volleys of gunfire like the ripping of some giant canvas, blasts from the cannon heaving one's stomach, nightmarish shrieks and groans, the telling spat when leaden balls hit human flesh…*SPAT!*

Shaken, he clutched at the window sash and listened: only the rainfall's low rushing sound. Daniel turned: his rain-soaked mack had fallen, slapping onto the wooden floor behind him. "Dammit…!" Blowing the oath through grit teeth, he shook his head to clear what remained of the vision. He walked back to the doorway, retrieved the coat and draped it instead across the rocker facing the fireplace. He knelt on the gray stone hearth and poked a splintered piece of kindling into the morning's coals and fanned the growing warmth back into the room; with it came the smell of bacon and charred hickory.

He bit at his lip. *No,* he thought. *Even on this hearth, I am far from home…* Of late, the blurry edge of exhaustion crowded his thoughts; between hellish dreams and the real threat of an invading Confederate

Army, Daniel had slept little. He closed his eyes and his hands clenched. *Get a hold…*

He stared into the growing flame, and another worry edged in. *It's late. And she's still not back...* Two days before, even as the battle raged in the valley, Sarah had gone to care for her father who was down with the fever. *That stubborn old fool,* he thought, *He'll never give up the ghost...* Old man Wagaman was a staunch Unionist; he and his son-in-law seldom agreed on anything, especially after Daniel resigned his commission. He frowned at his callousness. *No, she loves the old man, let him be; his time would come soon enough.* Then an odd, whispered admonition: *So may yours...* He shrugged off the dark thought, and realized the rekindled coals had singed his sleeve as he knelt thinking. Irritated, Daniel slapped at the sleeve and swore. *Dammit, get a hold!*

The quick tread on the porch stairs announced he was not alone. The door opened and Sarah bustled in, all shaking fabric and raindrops. She closed the door, put her valise and bags down, and started to remove her wet shawl. Daniel stood slowly and looked for her mood; hard to read these days, he thought, somehow very different. In their first years of marriage, they had settled into the soft intimacy of a childless couple, their calm routine gradually holding the unspoken worry that their union may be barren. When Sarah became pregnant after Daniel's first furlough home, a breath of fresh air came into their lives; their letters to each other welling with anticipation of what that new life would be.

He sighed deeply. *That sure as hell has changed...*

Shortly after he returned in the Spring, Sarah had miscarried. Broken-hearted, the couple had grown…quiet. Lately, Daniel's dark moods had drawn another curtain between them. *Nothing is the same...* He walked to the door and the two embraced – briefly. He spoke first.

"I was beginning to worry, Sarah... Everything all right?"

"I'm fine, Daniel. Just tired. It's just good to be home."

Sarah placed her wet shawl over the chair and turned with a sigh. She wore her auburn hair drawn back from her face in the tight bun that was in style; unconsciously, she tucked back the few wet strands that had fallen onto her temples. She looked careworn and exhausted; following the old trail that crossed Green Ridge above the farm, the journey from her parent's farm in the valley to the west was a rugged two-hour ride; if one had to be cautious, even longer. She looked around the room, then lifted her face to look at him.

"Everything's alright here?"

"So far, we're fine. Looks like the Rebs are pulling out of Gettysburg..."

"You mean it's over?" she interrupted, "They're gone? Do you think they burned the town? My parents haven't heard from Rebecca. Nothing at all. They are worried to death about her. They need you to..."

He put his hands on her arms, trying to calm her. "Don't get ahead of yourself. I don't know more than that, but I'm sure Becky is fine. Yes. Far as I can tell, Lee is headed into the passes. But how are your parents? Everyone is alright there?"

Sarah stopped to compose herself and started again. "Yes, Daniel, everyone there is safe. The Rebels seem to have missed their valley altogether. And my father was better today, so I thought it was time I came home." She turned to look out the porch window and knit her brow, gazing into the rain. "Mother let me their buggy to ride back in when the rain started so heavy. I left Tobey still hitched to it down in the shed. Isn't Lucius back yet?"

"Luke? Why, no. He's not..."

Daniel shook his head. No wonder there, he thought. Lucius and Anna Hand were the negro tenant farmers who really ran the Spencer farm while Daniel managed the family mill. With thousands of Secesh scouring the area, the Hands had hidden the previous week in the woods on the remote ridge above the farm. Luke was born a freeman, but his wife had made her way to the mountain on what was known as the Underground Railroad. Their birthrights made little difference: the Rebels were seizing all persons of color they came across and sending them south into slavery; Luke and Anna vowed to die before being taken.

Before they fled up the ridge, the Hands agreed to take most of the farm's livestock for safekeeping, a wagonload of foodstuff and grain – and Daniel's Henry repeating rifle. On the farm itself, Daniel kept enough to get by and keep the Rebel foragers occupied. His horse Tobey? Not the most handsome of animals to start with, the war had left the horse scarred and partially blind; Daniel purposely left the animal in the corral ungroomed and seemingly too far gone for use. The gambles had paid off. Few of the Southerners had found the obscure lane crossing the mountainside to the Spencer place; those that did requisitioned most of the remaining food and fodder, but the pitiful-looking gelding had not interested them. Since then, Sarah had made it safely to her parent's farm and back with the animal without incident. *But now, who knows...?* The anger rose from nowhere.

"Hell, Sarah. You were right next to the goddamn barn...you left the horse standing there out in the open? We just spent the past week trying to keep the damn Rebs from taking the animal! What were you thinking?"

Caught off guard, Sarah turned and looked at him, her mouth partly open with surprise. "I... Daniel, I'm tired and" she stopped. "Why are you so...angry?"

Daniel felt the blood rise in his face and he bit the inside of his cheek, but said nothing in reply. It went unspoken that he would have to hide the horse and carriage, and quickly: *any* form of transport was invaluable to a retreating army. Daniel headed to the door, and, with no little effort managed to get the wet leather boots back on his feet, and pulled the oilcloth over his head. Still livid, he began to slam the door behind him, then thought better of it. He closed it slowly, and stepped onto the porch. He stopped, his teeth clenched, closed his eyes, and thought. *What the hell is wrong with you?* The rain had slowed and he immediately caught the smell of fresh, wet, earth. *Antietam. Smells like the field at Antietam...*

He reopened his eyes and let the image go. Focusing on the carriage shed below, he started a smile; there, in the slow drizzle, Tobey and the rig still stood in the leaky structure, the horse looking forlornly toward the house. Daniel squinted down the lane – no Rebels in sight. He slogged across the puddled yard. Without unhitching the buggy, he untied Tobey from the shed, led him quickly into the barn, and closed the doors behind. Daniel went about unhitching the carriage traces, and pulling off the hames and collar, he walked the animal free.

He combed his fingers though the horse's wet forelock and looked him over; despite Daniel's attempts to leave Tobey in disarray, the Wagamans apparently had groomed the animal. Nonetheless, ugly purple scars still ran down the animal's flank. *Nothing's different about you, old man, you're homely as ever.* On his return from Virginia, Spencer found the injured horse at an Army slaughterhouse, healing, but too far-gone for military use. *Just like me...* In the months since, he had nursed the dispirited animal back to health; a clouded, almost sightless eye and deep scars remained, but he found the horse intelligent and surprisingly strong. Of late, Daniel found himself wondering whether his black moods didn't share some odd kinship with the animal's more visible scars. He wiped down the horse's coat and then led him to a stall with a measure of the remaining grain.

What to do with the Wagaman's buggy? *Nowhere else to hide it; it's as safe here as anywhere. If the Rebs come and find it after all this, so be it.* On the front seat of the carriage lay a shotgun, along with a napkin folded into a package. He found the shotgun held two fresh rounds; the napkin held three biscuits, one half–eaten, but still covered with cherry preserves. *Now that's Sarah's mother,* he thought. *Here, honey, take some biscuits and the shotgun for your ride home...*

Sarah's mother was an uncommon soul. The Wagamans were one of those hardy Dutch families who first settled the mountain – a shotgun and biscuits said it all. Sarah and her sister Rebecca were of this stock too, but the old man decided early on that his first daughter would be more refined, and sheltered her; so Sarah grew expecting life to be *just so*; her sister Rebecca was more willful than considered proper. *Another story entirely,* he thought. *But there was a time...* Daniel's thoughts ran on as he leaned against the buggy and ate the smaller piece of biscuit. *Damn that's good.* He re-wrapped the other pieces and stuffed the folded cloth under his mack.

He walked from the barn, and latching the door, glanced down the lane. *Oh hell...* Just a few yards down the path, a mounted figure in Confederate gray rode slowly toward him. Daniel fingered the folded papers in his pocket: hand-written receipts he received the first time the Rebs came through – he hoped to use them as proof the farm was already plundered.

As the rider came closer, Daniel's eyes moved to the faded gold braid on the man's sleeve that indicated an officer, and then to the long barrel of a pistol that lay across the horse's withers. Otherwise, the Southerner was motionless and alone; apparently on its own, his large black mare paced steadily up the lane, and halted by the water trough. Daniel winced: above where the man's left knee should have been, the leg ended in a thick wrap of soggy bandage; below the stained bandage, a stream of pale red drops ran from the saddle flap. Strapped around the Rebel's waist, a pair of leather belts held him in the saddle. *How the hell did he make it here...?*

Clearing his throat, the gray rider spoke barely above a whisper: "Sir, I would be obliged for some water..."

"Yes, of course. Can I...do you want some help down?"

"I'll stay as I am. Jest the water if you would."

Daniel took measure of the man: a single star lay on each side of the Rebel's collar. *A Major.* A broad hat kept much of the man's face in shadow, but piercing gray-blue eyes stared from under the brim. Not long ago, this Southerner must have cut a striking figure; a leader, someone you would follow. *Even into that hell...* Now, those eyes stared from hollow sockets, the once ruddy face was the color of withered grass. *John Dick had that look at Bull Run. This Reb likely doesn't have much time left...* Daniel's head throbbed. The quiet admonition came anew: *Neither may you. Help him.*

Daniel splashed up to the mouth of the cistern pipe that fed the trough, kneading his forehead. He filled a bucket, and gave a ladle–full to the

Southerner. *So this is the enemy...* He recalled the grim irony: even soaked to the skin, the wounded could never get enough water. *Help him...* He gestured toward the canteen hanging from the officer's saddle, and the Rebel nodded slightly. Daniel slowly untied the strap, filled the wooden container as well, and retied it to the saddle.

"Obliged, sir..."

"Name's Spencer. Are you hungry? Look, it's just biscuits, but..."

Keeping an eye to the Rebel's pistol, Daniel held one hand palm open in the air, and with the other slowly pulled the wrap holding the biscuits from under his coat. He held it up to the major, but the Southerner's gaze had shifted past him – with a flicker of interest, his eyes traced the fresh tracks in the mud leading to the barn. Daniel glanced over his shoulder and thought of the shotgun sitting on the carriage seat. Turning back, he found the officer staring at him. *No. Through me...* The Rebel looked briefly back to the tracks, but his curiosity had faded. The Southerner took the folded napkin and pushed it under his lapel flap.

"I am obliged, sir. I'll be on my way. God bless you." With that, and again with no apparent guidance, the Rebel's horse turned and plodded back down the lane into the gloom.

We're not all that different... Daniel remembered it all too well: the Yankee politicians had cried, "Restore the Union! Restore the Union!" After all was said and done, Spencer found that this war *restored* very little. His initiation to battle came at Second Bull Run; there, a newly-minted general had bungled his orders, and the Pennsylvanians had been shot to pieces. Among the dead was the company captain, John Dick, and Spencer rose to command. *Even promotion rides on a dead man's back...* Then came the slaughter at Antietam; the wounds from that day still pained him. Soon after, there was the disaster at Fredericksburg: more bungling, more slaughter, and another wound. In the weeks that followed Fredericksburg, the outer injury had healed well enough, but something within him had changed. *There is no end to this; everything I do gets good men killed – for what? Senseless. With all of them dead, why am I alive?* Disgusted, mentally and physically spent, Spencer took a military discharge that winter. Perhaps returning to his home and family would restore his perspective, his humanity.

He found respite at first; but in time, the closer he came to reclaiming the old life, the more distant it became. A good part of him wanted to avoid the matter entirely: leave the farm, disappear into the wooded ridges of the mountain. There he could live a recluse life and never have to deal with men or their folly again. But nightmares started soon after, exhaustion added to a gnawing sense of isolation, and even the energy to leave fell out of reach. Of late, dark images had crept in to his waking hours. *And the horror follows…*

The rain turned heavy again. Spencer closed his eyes and twisted his head side to side relieve the tension in his neck. Still keeping an eye down the lane, he retrieved the shotgun from the barn and splashed back to the house. The front door was partially ajar, and Sarah peered out. Her father had filled her with horrific stories about the rumored cruelty of these Rebels, and now she stood, eyes wide, and a hand clenched to her mouth.

"Oh my God, Daniel...what did he want?" Her voice was shaking. She opened the door wider, but he stood motionless on the porch and said nothing. His head down, he stared down at the wooden threshold; the empty look in the Rebel's eyes still haunted him. *Might as well be me. Even on this doorstep, I am far from home...*

"Daniel...?"

He looked up, gazing past Sarah into the room beyond. He spoke distantly, "The man just needed water. He's gone."

"But... Did he see the carriage? He'll bring more Rebels back, won't he? It's all my fault, isn't it?"

He turned and stared back down the lane; the anger rose again. "Oh hell, Sarah. Enough! It's over. It wasn't your fault. Don't be foolish, that Reb looked to be half-dead. Do you really think he'll be coming back? Enough!"

Spencer shook out the wet coat, and pushing by her, stepped back inside. He put the scattergun on the mantel, and stared at the coals below. Her eyes downcast, Sarah closed the door behind him, and then leaned with her back against the dark wood, closing out the downpour.

"Daniel...."

He turned and looked. Calmer now, Sarah still leaned with her back to the door, her eyes fixed on him. In happier times, the depth of her blue eyes had first attracted him; now those eyes welled with tears, and their color was all the deeper. Exhausted, her remaining strength drained by the scare, Sarah had nothing left to stop the heartache that came to the surface; her voice still unsteady, but this time with frustration and sorrow.

"I don't know...if I can do this anymore. I need to know what's wrong. I thought you might feel better if...if we were apart for a few days, but you're worse – we're worse. I said I was sorry about Tobey. I don't know what else to do..."

She turned toward him, more settled now. She lifted her chin, and tried to steady her voice.

"Daniel. I need to know what's wrong. You barely sleep. You're cross with me all the time, but why? You won't talk about it – is it me? Is it losing the baby? Is it? What would you have me do? I have been through enough... You need to tell me what's happening. If not..." Sarah bit off her words and turned away.

Daniel looked silently about the beamed ceiling as if some answer lay in the shadows of the dark wood. He started quietly. "Sarah, it's not anything you can fix. It's nothing I can even put a finger on." He turned to the window and stared back into the downpour. "I lived through all that. The battles, the wounds, even the damn hospitals... I survived. Couldn't wait to get home, back to our life here. Well, here I am, but something has changed. It feels wrong; I feel wrong. Something is..." His voice rose and his head pounded.

"Hell, what do you want me to tell you? I don't know what's wrong! Maybe there is no goddamn problem; maybe there is no coming home..."

He caught himself. He was angry again. Sarah was crying. *There is no coming home....* Behind Sarah's quiet sobs, Daniel could hear the rain on the porch roof. *Stop...* He stood gripping the windowsill for a long moment, but then turned.

"I can tell you this: that all that time, getting back to you was all that kept me going. And now I'm driving you away..."

"You haven't driven me away," she sobbed, "Can't you see I'm trying to understand?"

She moved closer. She stood stiffly at first, unsure, but leaned against him. His arms closed around her as the tears came. For some time they held each other, warm and close. But something was still missing... *Even in this house, in her arms, I am not home...*

Daniel opened his eyes, his gaze shifted out the porch window again. The rain had slowed some and wisps of fog rose from the hillside. A chill grew in the pit of his stomach. *Just like Antietam...*

September 17, 1862: Morning
West of Antietam Creek, Maryland

The light of early morning had just turned the North Woods a somber green when gunfire broke out again. Filtering their way through the trees, a broad column of blue-coated soldiers stopped at the southern edge of the woods; officers moved back and forth along the line, encouraging, straightening the ranks. In their front, freshly plowed ground stretched south to a meadow and a field of corn, the tall stalks ready for harvest. The overnight rain had finally tapered off; streaks of fog rose slowly, drifting wraiths above the dark furrowed soil.

Midway back in the formation, the lieutenant blew sweat off the end of his nose. The regiment stood two companies wide and five deep, in what the manual called *Column of Divisions... Yes,* he thought, *it keeps two hundred-odd souls together, but these woodlots raise hell keeping order.* Spencer glanced down the line of Company B; their ranks were not in bad shape. He squinted up into the canopy of leaves overhead. *Who was it they said owned this farm? Poffenberger? A Dutchman. Sounds almost like home...* Conveniently, he thought, between gathering firewood and grazing cattle, these old German farmers left just enough room in their woods to maneuver.

He lifted his head and breathed in the damp air. *Besides, lately we don't take up much space...* He pulled off his cap, ran his fingers back through the wet hair, and closed his eyes. *One hundred and ninety left in the old 107th...and only twenty of Company B.* Then the thought came again: *And if I not up to it, I'll get them all killed...* He tugged the cap back tight on his head, and pulled up at the knapsack straps cramping his shoulders.

Spencer craned his neck to see what was happening beyond the woods; ahead, Captain MacThompson and an aide rode slowly at the edge of the treeline, peering across the field as a late summer sun rose to light the

furrows. Then it started: the occasional, almost measured *zzz-ip* of a Minie'
ball. *Odd. Not really a ball at all,* Spencer thought. Just an ounce or so of
bullet-shaped lead; but fired from a rifled musket in knowing hands, it
defined how resourceful men had become at killing one another.

We're not in range yet – just some Reb hoping to get lucky...

A stir erupted in the woods behind and a mounted courier raced by the
column. Scattering horse sweat and clods of earth, the rider slid his lathered
animal to a stop on the wet ground in front of MacThompson. The rider
saluted.

"Sir. Compliments of General Duryea. He would like your regiment to
move with the brigade to the edge of yonder cornfield, form line of battle,
and advance to cooperate with Meredith's Brigade on the right. The balance
of the Division will follow in support."

The courier wiped his face with his hand, glanced out of the tree line
and then back at MacThompson. He saluted and said, "With all due respect
sir, been hearing there is the devil's muster of Rebels beyond that corn..."
With that, the rider turned his horse and raced through the trees to the next
regiment. The Captain returned the salute, and stared across the field; he
spurred his horse to the head of the column.

"Attention! Skirmish companies to the front! On the right, take
intervals!"

Down the line, others echoed the order, and about thirty men cleared the
sides of the column, fanned out into a thin line, and moved across the
plowed field. MacThompson then bellowed, "107th Pennsylvania! Forward
at the common step! March!"

The compact formation headed out of the treeline across the open
ground at a walk, and the distant pop of gunfire grew, ticking at the wet air;
for the moment, their missiles whined overhead. Breathing harder, Spencer
coughed at the thick smell of wet, fresh-plowed earth. Now he could see

across the field: beyond the cornstalks was what looked to be a white schoolhouse sat on the rise in the distance, and in front of it…a long line of Rebel cannon belching white smoke. *Oh God, here it comes…* A second later, the thumps of the big guns rolled over the field, and immediately after, flame and hot metal burst overhead, tearing through the air above the regiment. Spencer dodged at the blast; around him, a hundred blue caps stooped in unison. *Like some sermon in hell.*

"Lookout boys," crowed a private in the front rank, "it's another goddamn shooting gallery."

It was indeed: to their left, members of the other regiments did their best to dodge the round shot and bursting shells as they skirted another patch of woods. On the right, a man-high shelf of rock cut the path of the advance, and funneled the Pennsylvanians into a bowl-shaped plain. Instinctively, they began to move faster. Spencer winced. Hadn't taken long for the boys to learn about artillery: a man is totally vulnerable – powerless – under cannonfire, and the effects so *random*. To underscore the thought, hot iron hissed noisily by his ear and the man behind him let out a shriek, and then silently collapsed into the soft earth. With a loud crack, another twelve-pound cannonball landed directly in front of the regiment, smashed one of the limestone outcroppings that cut the field, then bounded over the formation; then another explosion, a spray of crimson blushed the air in the front rank, and a sergeant from the color guard fell in a heap into the men behind. *Powerless...*

Hellish blasts of sulfur and screaming metal swatted down at the packed ranks from each side. Spencer's mind raced: *Sonofabitch! That was close...we're sitting ducks, another damn Bull Run.* He shook his head and tried to organize his thoughts: *We're still in one piece...just keep moving; this part is the worst...move, move, move!* He heard his voice, "Stay in line, boys. Keep moving!"

Moments crossing the field became a collage of horrid images overlaid with blasts of flame, gasped breath, rattling equipment, and tramping feet. *How long since we left the woods?* Maybe a minute? But how long is that? *How many dead men make up a minute?*

Just short of the cornfield the column slowed, the officers bellowed more orders, and the brigade began to shift into a two–ranked battle line. To his left, the lieutenant could see the other three regiments of Duryea's Brigade, all New York boys, wheeling into formation as if on parade. The line came to a halt at the edge of the corn. Spencer took a brief look at his company again: ashen faces with taut mouths stared back at him, but miraculously, most had made it across.

"So far so good, L'tenit." Sergeant Quinn had appeared at his elbow. "Rebs have a pile of artillery yonder, but I'll bet only a few guns really got the range on us. And looks like now they have other fish to fry."

He recalled the moments crossing the field. *Only a few...?* Spencer looked back over the ground behind them: the furrowed puddles of rainwater lay trampled into a costly avenue of mud. Every few feet lay a blue-clad figure, some writhing, some still; barely recognizable shapes more horrid lay in their midst. He turned from the scene and closing his eyes, tried to erase the image. Either way, Quinn was right: the Southern guns had found another target for the moment.

He looked past the sergeant down the ranks: the four regiments stood ready in a straight front that covered some 400 yards. *Impressive...* More orders were bellowed: knapsacks were passed to the rear and put in stacks. *But this is it. This time we will beat them...* He nodded to himself. *I can make a difference...* Moments later, more orders were relayed down the line from officer to officer: "Battalion! Charge Bayonets!"

With a shout, the front rank lowered their muskets from their shoulders to hip level; as the long line of rifles swung down, the lieutenant watched the long, triangular blades clipping at the tall stalks in their front. Above the pounding of his heart, he heard MacThompson's voice, "107th Pennsylvania! Guide on the colors! Forward at the route step! March!"

With that, hundreds of glistening bayonets pushed into the cornfield, the broad leaves trembling as the plants fell underfoot. Spencer pushed on through the stalks, a loud ringing pressed in his ears; he shook his head to clear it, and drew his Colt pistol. He heard himself bellowing, "Steady, boys. Keep moving…"

Spencer walked on and brushed aside the thick leaves. Then Rebel rifles opened from somewhere ahead; time seemed to slow and his thoughts fragmented with the scene around him. A hiss, a flat *ssluck*, and the private to his left front spun to the ground, wrapped in a shroud of leaves. *Spat*, then came the thud of another nameless soul hitting the ground. Shredded by bullets, then trampled into the earth, the stalks began to give off the wholesome smell of freshly shucked corn. With each impact, a flash of the morning's sky opened briefly amid the shattered plants. His thoughts became a tangle of the colliding images. *Bright green leaves, dark red blood, perfect hell under blue sky.* In counterpoint to the churning violence below, he could see their regimental flag, a red and blue shroud gliding gently across the top of the yet unbroken stalks.

At last, the tangled cornfield gave way to open ground on the south side of the field. There, the now ragged battle line found a snake rail fence and stopped; those in front began to pull down the upper rails. Free of the tall stalks, Spencer lifted his pistol and squinted to get a clear view of what lay ahead. Another broad meadow lay to the south; beyond, the sun had burned off some of the mist and the Rebel cannon were plainly visible by the squat white building in the distance. He waited his turn to cross the rails, calmly trying to count the number of Southern cannon; abruptly, his view was interrupted: a long line of gray and butternut uniforms rose from the underbrush just fifty yards across the meadow. He could hear their officers bellowing orders; on command, hundreds of rifles swung down, leveled toward the blue figures struggling to cross the rail fence. *Oh God...*

"Take cover! Down! Get the hell down!"

With a low, ripping crash, a cloud of gray-white smoke rolled toward Spencer's line, and those still standing at the fence fell as grass under a scythe. *Goddammit!* "Fire!" Spencer shouted, "Fire at will, goddammit!" Their first scattering of shots grew into a crash as the gunfire spread down the line. Several missiles zipped around him, one tugging at his sleeve. *Cover. Find some cover...* He heard his own voice through the roar, "Company B! Back behind the fence! Take cover!"

Through the smoke, he could make out Sergeant Quinn moving along the line pulling men back behind the fence rails, and bellowing encouragement.

"That's the way to do it, laddie! Pour it into 'em. Aim low, boys!"

Amidst the din, an indistinguishable mix of curses and prayers rose and fell, but gradually the sounds melded with the buzzing ring in Spencer's head. Thick white smoke hung in the moist air, further numbing the senses. During it all, in the back of his thoughts, *Why aren't I hit? I don't feel anything...* The lieutenant knelt behind the rails and peered below the waist-high cloud; beneath, he could only make out the legs of the Rebels in the pasture beyond – and the bodies of those dropping to the ground. He aimed his pistol into the cloud above one pair of legs, and squeezed the trigger three times. He lifted his head to see clear of the pistol's smoke: the body above the limbs collapsed, a lifeless gray uniform in the tall grass, his face a mass of crimson. *One dead Reb...* Again he raised the pistol, firing into the haze until the Colt's hammer clucked on an empty cylinder. He couldn't tell if his other shots hit their mark; the bile rose in his throat all the same. *I killed a man. Some mother's son...*

Spencer swallowed hard, knelt on one knee, and set about reloading. The image of the Rebel soldier falling streamed through his mind. *You killed him...* While he loaded, he glanced down the ranks again. As if part of a dream, his men loaded their weapons mechanically, hoisting the long muskets to their shoulders – the shot lost in the din – but their bodies jolting with the recoil, then starting the process again. There was no way to tell how much time had passed. *Time flies on slow wings when Death comes calling...*

Above it all, the color-sergeant hoisted the striped National flag; its folds fell limp in the damp, smoky air. Spencer loaded the last chamber of the Colt, watching blankly as Rebel bullets plucked at the fabric of the banner like invisible fingers. The very air seemed alive; bullets buzzed and hissed into the cornstalks behind him. Still, in the back of his thoughts: *Why aren't I hit...?*

Luck seemed to be his alone: a flat thud came from Spencer's left, and spurting blood, a carpenter from Chambersburg blew back into the man behind him. Then the color-sergeant toppled over, pulling the flag down with him. Another soldier stepped up to lift the banner and just as quickly dropped, and the now stained colors fell back into the smashed corn stalks. Out of the haze, another figure appeared and hoisted the flag again; the acrid smoke burned Spencer's eyes and nose. *Hard to goddamn breathe...* He squinted to see: *J.D. That crazy Irish kid...* Word had it Johnny Delaney had lied about his age to enlist, and had turned all of fourteen-years old while in camp that April. *So much for youth...* The boy hoisted the flag yet again. Just then, another man dropped with a moan at Spencer's feet, a bullet through his shoulder. *Good God... Damn Rebs have us pinned. We need to move...forward?* Beyond the fence, the rain of missiles was an unseen boundary. *Do something!*

Then he felt it: an odd pause in the buzzing chaos; a breath held and slowly exhaled, a barely felt breeze shifting direction; something was changing. Sergeant Quinn appeared, red-faced and wagging his hand to the right – he was yelling something, but his voice made no sound. The lieutenant pressed his hands to his temples to clear his head. He stared blankly at the sergeant. *What...?* Quinn grabbed Spencer's arm and bellowed in his ear.

"L'tenit! Somethin's wrong. I don't see any of the regiments to our right! Goddamn if we are not flanked!"

Spencer looked numbly beyond Quinn. Through the thick smoke he could see little, only shadows and bursts of orange flame, but the right of the company was turning and firing to the west. *What the hell...?*

At the same moment, Jim Corcoran, the lieutenant of the company to their left, ran up and shouted, "Spence! I'll be damned if the rest of the brigade hasn't withdrawn. There's Rebs all over my left flank! I am pulling back!" Corcoran turned and ran back into the smoke to his men.

Spencer knelt down, trying to focus. *We can't withdraw. There are no orders to fall back...* But through the haze where Corcoran disappeared, more orange streaks of flame now stretched toward them. *Our own damn officers left us behind again... Do something!*

Quinn pulled at Spencer's arm. "L'tenit...?"

"Goddammit! Orders or no. Let's get the hell out of here!" Spencer turned and yelled down the line: "Company B! Fall back firing! Now! Quinn! You know what to do!"

The sergeant waved a salute, and dashed along the line, yelling, tugging at shoulders and collars to make himself understood in the roar. When all those that could still move had started back, Quinn turned and nodded to the lieutenant. Spencer fired his last round, then quickly stood and turned to sprint into the corn stalks. A blow to the right side of his ribcage knocked him sprawling into the leaves. The lieutenant lay motionless, face first in the moist earth, the spinning roar around him fading into a quiet void.

All was quite dark when Daniel awoke with a start; his side ached still as he lay in the gloom alone. He was drained and, despite the warm air that surrounded him, he lay in a cold sweat. He had dreamt of home, but the remaining vision quickly dissolved into images of the battle. *Sarah... No. Just another dream...* With that, the familiar sense of dread came rushing back. *Antietam...* He could hear a quiet rustling from the corn stalks nearby; he started as the noise sounded again, this time right beside him. "Quinn...?" He opened his eyes; a warm glow from a glass lamp chased at the darkness.

"No Daniel, it's me. Sarah. You're home."

What the hell? His thoughts swirled. He sat up slowly and pressed his palms to his eyes. *God, what is happening? How is she here?* Sarah knelt, put the lamp on the floor, and pulled him against her. *Warm and soft...*

"Daniel, you were having a dream – a nightmare. Wake up...you're home. You fell asleep in front of the fireplace; you seemed exhausted, so I let you sleep. But I've been right here in the chair. You're home now..."

"Sarah..." He said it carefully just to hear the name. He shook his head to clear the remaining vision. "That was no dream. It was real."

Sarah looked at him, her face flushed red from the warm hearth and lined with concern. She whispered quietly, "No Daniel, you're home now. What's happening to you? These memories – is it the Rebels being here that's brought them back? I want to help you. You're home now..." She then leaned back and peered into his face as she held him, looking for him to believe.

Daniel tried to clear his thoughts. Her face came into focus. *Blue eyes in the dawn... But that was long ago. It's all different now...*

"Sarah. I'm so sorry, sorry to be the cause of more heartache for you. This is not your fault. Something just isn't right. I will need to find my way somehow. Wherever I am now, I am not *home*..."

No more words to say, Sarah leaned back, her lips pressed tightly together, her eyes welling. She rose and went to the kitchen. Daniel could hear the steps creak as she went to the springhouse below. He stood slowly and stretched, walked to the front door and stepped onto the porch; he stared into the darkness. The light from inside shimmered in the steady stream of rainwater that ran off the eave, but the scarce pattering on the roof said the downpour had let up. From the fields below, a slight breeze blew in the thick smell of rich earth and wet corn.

Antietam...

September 17, 1862: Morning
West of Antietam Creek, Maryland

Consciousness came with the low hum in his ears, and the sound swelled like rolling thunder. He haltingly lifted his head from the wet earth and blew the dirt from his nose and mouth; a tangled knot of green leaves and stalks wrapped his legs. The rest of his body lay stunned; any effort to draw a full breath drew an agonizing cough. He tried again; as his lungs filled, a searing pain ran up his side. Spencer moved his hand down and prodded his ribs to feel for the bloody hole; the touch sent another wave of agony through him, but there was no evidence of the injury he expected. Part of his brain told him the wound wasn't bad, but the gripping pain left him paralyzed. No recognizable sounds met his ears over the buzzing roar that had taken over; he shook his head to try to clear the chaos of his thoughts. *I've failed... Gotten us shot to pieces.* Just then, there was tugging at the shoulders of his uniform, and in more agony, he felt himself being dragged up from the tangle.

"Come on L'tenit. Hell of a place to take a breather! We need to go. Can you walk?"

Quinn. It's goddamn Quinn... With all his strength, Spencer stood and leaning on the Sergeant, pushed one foot after another into the earth, stumbling through what remained of the cornfield. The movement brought burning gasps of sulfurous air into his lungs; even so, he felt his senses start to focus. They finally broke from the stalks into the meadow near where the brigade had first formed its line.

Only then did he understand their loss: a few hundred men from various units milled about, some reforming on their flag or an officer, others helped badly wounded comrades to the rear. Several men seemed beside themselves from shock, staring off into the ruined corn, whispering silently, or jabbering nonsense. Spencer took in shallow breaths to keep from heaving.

He gasped at the Sergeant. "Quinn...this won't do! Need to find the regiment...get the company together."

"I'm with you there, sir." He shouted, "I'll sees who I can find. Can you stand on your own?"

He stood clear of the sergeant: he was wobbly and his side throbbed like hell, but he was upright - it would do; he nodded to Quinn, and the sergeant ran off. Spencer squinted along the edge of the corn: there stood young Delaney and the regiment's national flag, but there were few familiar faces nearby. He hobbled over and put his hand on the boy's shoulder.

"J.D., is this everyone? Where's the 107th...?"

The youngster looked vacantly at him, and slowly saluted. The words came out between gulps of air. "Well sir...it's meself; and these here fellows...they're from Company A... I think that's 'C' over there...and

there's your company. I ain't seen anyone else. The rest of the brigade is...
Somewhere. I don't know. But I'm here, sir."

Spencer squinted at the youth: Delaney stood shaking, unaware of the
tears that streaked the black powder on his cheeks, or the dark stain that wet
the front of his trousers, but defiant and still clutching the staff of the blood-
spattered flag tightly with both hands. *Crazy, fearless kid...*

"Good job, J.D. For now, we'll reform here on the colors." The
lieutenant looked about: seven or eight from his company stood or knelt off
to one side, some staring blankly at the ground; in all, he could see perhaps
thirty men of the regiment. Quinn came limping back.

"Well, L'tenit, it's bad, but not as bad as it looks. We only got this few
here, but the rest of the regiment is back there by the woods. Looks to be
that General Duryea ordered the brigade out of that cornfield a while ago;
but only part of our boys got the message. Just like Bull Run, a'course. Us,
and Company 'A,' and Lt. Corcoran's 'C,' we was all left behind; and well,
we caught the worst of it. Looks like about half the boys are down."

The lieutenant stared at Quinn. *Half...? That can't be. We weren't there
but a few min...* Looking up, Spencer squinted: the sun was well into the
sky, at least an hour or two had passed since sunrise. *My God. I wanted to
make a difference... I did. I've gotten us shot all to hell.* Out of the glare, a
rider trotted across the meadow toward them: Captain MacThompson. He
waved a salute and eyed Spencer. The Captain yelled over the renewed roar
that rolled in from the far side of the cornfield.

"Lieutenant Spencer. Are you alright?" He looked about at the few men
around the flag. "My God, this is all you have left?"

The grating hum in the lieutenant's ears still came and went; he guessed
at the Captain's words, gave a weak salute and nodded. MacThompson
steadied his mount and shouted again.

"I'm sure you heard what goddamn happened. These fool generals…" The Captain caught himself, but then continued. "Well, anyway… If it helps, the Rebs you fought retreated. They had to bring up another two brigades just to hold that line. Well done, Lieutenant. Our brigade is reforming back at that treeline across the field. Pass the word and meet up with the rest of the regiment there."

Still clutching his side, Spencer saluted as the captain galloped off. He stared down absently at the reddish mud that crusted his boots, then pressed his hands to his eyes. *The Rebs brought up two brigades to hold that line. Well done…* The lieutenant looked up to see what remained of the company and wasn't sure how *well* he had done. *Well done? I got us shot all to hell… And we're back where we started…* He closed his eyes and shook his head. Jim Corcoran limped over, his hat gone and his face streaked with gunpowder.

"Spence…damn, are you alright? I just saw Quinn; my boys caught hell too. Bad. Looks like this is everybody, everybody that's left anyway. You ready to move?"

"Yeah – ready as we'll get, Corcoran. Let's get 'em moving…"

A dull sun shone through the smoke in the mid-day sky; what remained of the three companies rejoined the regiment inside the same woods where they had paused at dawn. The handful that remained of the company stacked arms and collapsed on the muddy turf. Some huddled around small fires, boiling coffee and discussing the morning's fight; others sat quietly and kept to themselves.

The lieutenant leaned against a tall pine, and turned to look for Quinn; as usual, the sergeant appeared beside him. "Lookin' for me, sir…? You alright?"

"Shit, Quinn!" He started a small laugh, but a sharp pain turned it to a gasp. "And yes, I'm passable. Be a damn sight better if everyone stopped asking me if I was alright."

The Sergeant was looking at him curiously, his head cocked and his eyebrows raised. "Well, L'tenit, if you could see yourself…"

Spencer finally took a moment to check his wound. *What the hell…?* From the look of it, the blow he felt in his side had been a piece of shell: his belt strap was cut almost in half; under the gashed leather was a gaping hole in the blue wool; beneath, his shirt pocket showed a singed black ring where gunpowder and hot iron had burned through the cloth. He pulled open the jacket buttons and pulled back the flap. Inside the burnt pocket was a packet an inch or so thick and tied with cord: Sarah's letters. Many of the men chose to destroy letters from home; rather that, than they possibly fall under the derisive gaze of some enemy. Spencer had chosen to keep Sarah's mail – not so much out of optimism as an inexplicable hesitation. Now Spencer pulled out the packet, and was stunned to see an ugly shard of dark iron piercing the middle of the bundle. He carefully put the packet down and pulled open his shirt. An angry dark crimson welt showed where his ribs had absorbed the hit. He shook his head in disbelief.

Quinn wagged his head. "Well, sir, I heard tell of a man bein' saved like that, but never seen it. Don't that beat all?"

Then the sergeant fixed his gaze on Spencer's hat and nodded. He pulled off his cap: a bullet hole showed just above the front brim, and exited the back. As if to confirm the near-miss, Spencer ran his hand through his hair and found a small crease crossing his scalp; absent-mindedly, he wiped at the trickle of blood that ran from his hairline. In the meantime, several of the company had gathered around the lieutenant: enthusiastically, they pointed out the holes in both of his sleeves, one trouser leg, and yet another through his collar.

Spencer was stunned. "Damn, looks like someone's trying to kill me…"

The group laughed nervously: death was still too close. Assured that Spencer was indeed in one piece, the men began to sit down nearby in small groups. The lieutenant suddenly felt drained, and leaning against the pine trunk, slowly slid to the ground. *I've gotten us shot all to hell...*

A medical attendant appeared and started working his way through the regiment's wounded. Eventually the soldier, a somewhat grimy corporal with a green chevron on his sleeve and a dark-stained medical valise, noticed Spencer leaning against the tree and walked over. He gave a half-hearted salute and eyed the gash in Spencer's uniform. He said indifferently, "Sir, I should probably take a look – if you don't mind…"

The lieutenant nodded assent and leaned back; as the corporal poked and prodded his side, Spencer silently noted the dried blood and dirt that outlined the attendant's wrinkled skin and fingernails. The man's eyes fell on the iron-torn bundle of letters that lay in the lieutenant's lap.

"That's what stopped the shell? Well, I'll be damned. Lieutenant, I tell you what: if your wife loved you any less, you'd be a dead man. But judgin' from the size of that hunk of iron, I'm bettin' you cracked a rib or two at least. Best to wrap you up."

Spencer glared at the soldier, but took his meaning. He waved the attendant off. "I'll be fine, corporal, look to these other men…"

The corporal shrugged, "Yassir…" He gave another vague salute, and moved on to the next wounded man.

Finally left to himself, Spencer shuddered at the close call. *If your wife loved you any less, you'd be a dead man…* Odd, he thought, how one's very life could turn on some random item: a bundle of letters from home. *Maybe not so random…* The smell of woodsmoke and coffee grounds crept into his thinking. *Home…* He breathed in deeply, but a quick spasm of pain cut his breath. He leaned around the tree. A few feet away, a soldier in a muddy blue tunic fanned a wood fire; suspended above, a pot of coffee was starting to boil; small drops spilled over, hissing as they fell into the embers below.

July 4, 1863: Night
South Mountain, Pennsylvania

He sat by the stone hearth, raking at the coals with the poker; something in the warm glow of the embers seemed to edge out the empty chill the images left in their wake. He stood and stretched. On the mantle in front of him sat several daguerreotypes cased in dark gutta-percha. Daniel found the glass photographs as wearisome as they were unique: like a mirage on hot macadam, the substance of the image came and went according to the way one viewed it. *Much like our lives...*

He moved his head to one side, and the light reflected on a likeness of him just the year before. A few weeks after muster, a photographer erected a makeshift tent studio in a tent, and for two dollars, a soldier could have his image made for his loved ones. A crudely painted mural formed the background for all: a stylized army camp with a line of tents in rough perspective, what would have been an enormous American flag waving overhead. Unlike many of the newly-minted officers, Lieutenant Spencer had opted not to stand formally at attention for the photograph. The image showed him sitting, albeit stiffly, his dark hair brushed to one side with his kepi in his lap. His intention had been to appear determined, but during the long exposure, he had moved his head, the effect made for a less certain demeanor.

"You'd feel better if you would eat something."

He turned. Sarah had appeared from the kitchen and placed some platters on the table where they shared their meals. In the floating shadows cast by the lamp, she sliced pieces from a small ham, and laid them on honey bread; she went back to the kitchen and returned with a crock of sweet potatoes from the bake-oven, and ladled them steaming onto the plate beside the bread. Daniel stared at the small feast, shaking his head in disbelief: the Rebels had fairly scoured everything from their kitchen and the springhouse below.

"Where did you get...?"

She looked at him and started a smile. "Mother sent it along," she said, then pretended a frown, "You know how she thinks you're thin."

Daniel nodded; taking a seat, he ate heartily, but in silence. Across the table, Sarah watched him, deep in thought. The food seemed to help; pale and distant when he first sat down, the food seemed to restore something in him. He looked up at her and nodded slowly.

"Your mother is an angel. Now. What's this about your sister?"

She looked at him quickly, pensive. "I wasn't sure if you heard me. My parents are worried to death about Rebecca. Even at their farm yesterday, we could hear the cannon from the valley. They thought she might come home, but there's been no word; she must still be in Gettysburg. But how can we go looking for her now? And you've been...well, you're exhausted. It will have to wait."

As he ate, Daniel thought to himself. *Rebecca...* Becky was more independent, more like her mother. Two years before, she had left home and accepted a position teaching in Gettysburg. *No surprise there; she and the old man just don't see things the same way...* That was where Daniel had met the Wagaman sisters. Daniel had first courted Becky. *Independent as all hell...* Their relationship had been intense but brief; as it happened, it also eventually led to his engagement to her sister Sarah. Now Daniel looked at her thoughtfully.

"Waiting may be a good idea," he said. "Until we know more of what's happened, I can't see much we can do. You know how I *hate* to disagree with your father, but..."

Sarah frowned. Daniel shrugged and continued, "In spite of what your father believes, I don't think the Southerners would harm a woman. And

53

Becky's a smart girl; she'd find a safe place during the fighting. If the town is in one piece, she should be okay. For the moment, all we can do is wait and see."

The couple finished their meal in silence, and then without discussion, began a long-established routine: while Sarah cleared the meal, Daniel went out to tend to the animals for the night, at the moment, only his horse Tobey.

The storm began again in earnest as he reached the barn entrance. Inside, the rain rattled drum-like on the shingled roof. He lit the oil lamp that hung inside the door and gazed around the still interior. He heard Sarah's words. *You're fine now...* But his head throbbed; before him in the flickering shadows was an image. Shrouded in dark smoke and fire, a figure in Confederate gray lay on the ground. *Antietam. The first man I killed; some mother's son. And how many more...* The wavering light showed another bloodied figure, then another - a barnful of dead men. A revulsion rose in Daniel's chest: not at the gore, but at himself.

He closed his eyes and held his palms to the pounding at his temples. He looked up; he was still at the doorway, alone in the dark. The images were gone, only the familiar earthy scent of the old barn drifted in the wet air. He rubbed his eyes with thumb and forefinger and turned up the lamp flame. He exhaled a long breath, went to the spare stall, retrieved a sack of grain that he had hidden under the floorboard, and headed to the Tobey's stall. The horse turned and nickered quietly.

"Well, old man. It's just you and me tonight. Sorry about the short rations today; maybe we'll let you graze tomorrow. Things will get back to normal soon."

His words died quickly in the damp air. *Maybe...*

The horse ate intently while Daniel stood silent, staring into the shadows while he slowly rubbed the animal's neck. *It's over. I need to forget...* He sighed, and lifting the lantern from the shelf, headed to the doorway. *Things will get back to normal soon...* Tobey turned, looked at him briefly and turned back to his grain.

Closing the wooden door behind, Spencer stopped and leaned back against the wet boards, trying to clear his head. The rain was starting to let up, even so a few drops still rolled off the brim of his hat; across the yard, amber candlelight flickered in the deep-set windows of the stone house. Closing his eyes, he took in a deep breath: the cool air was thick with moisture and the smell of the mountain at night. *You're fine now...* He took his time crossing the yard, walking slowly, taking in the growing calm. He climbed the porch, and again started to shake the water from his coat. Wet as it was, he gave a laugh at the effort; he draped the mack on the porch rail and opened the door.

Inside, the still darkness wandered in the flame of a single candle by the staircase. He looked at the ceiling and listened, he could hear Sarah's bare feet padding around the second floor. He nodded another sigh, and in the

55

waving shadows, pulled off his soaked boots and set them to dry. He blew out the candle, climbed the stairs in the dark, and walked quietly into their bedroom. In the corner, Sarah was rinsing her face at the nightstand. He watched as she studied her face in the mirror above the basin. She noticed him watching, and started a self-conscious smile; she turned toward him.

"Everything alright?"

"Yes, everything's fine." He reassured himself. *You're fine now...*

Sarah placed the towel on the stand to dry and walked to him. She hesitated, then gently ran her fingers over his cheekbones. "We'll work this out, Daniel. But now, you look exhausted," she said softly. "Maybe you'll sleep better tonight."

He stood silently gazing into the lamp, his thoughts stalled. *Exhausted.* Sarah unbuttoned his shirt, pulled it back off his shoulders, and folded it over the chair by the door. He walked to the nightstand to wash up, and gazed into the mirror. Lately, the face that stared back at him was so unlike the image he expected, he wondered why Sarah did not recoil at this stranger in their home. His face had grown haggard and dark circles lay under his eyes. *Used up. Empty...* He was still staring in the mirror when he heard Sarah come up behind him. She looked to him.

"Come to bed, Daniel."

"Sarah. I need to say something. I know I've been selfish, thoughtless when you needed me most..." She put her hand to his lips.

"We'll get through this. We will do this one day at a time." She looked down for a moment, thinking on her words; then turned and walked to the bed, pulling him with her.

Daniel sat down on the edge of the mattress, watching Sarah intently, as if she might suddenly disappear. She sat beside him and took his hands in hers. She smiled and said softly, "Everything will be fine. Get some sleep." She blew out the lamp, and lay back, pulling the spread over her. His eyes were heavy; he stretched out beside her; he tried to sort the day's events into perspective, but soon dozed off.

It was well into the night when he awoke, his head aching again. Something was terribly wrong. *What? You're fine now. You are home…* He slid back the coverlet, and sat up on the side of the bed, pressing his palms to his forehead. He turned and looked behind him. The moon, just past full, had broken the thick clouds and shone brightly though the window. Sarah lay on her side snoring slightly, one arm tucked under her head, the other reaching out across Daniel's pillow. In her sleep, she had thrown back the coverlet; her nightgown rested high on her thighs, and her long legs lay blue-white in the moonlight. *Beautiful.* He felt his heart pounding. *But something is very…wrong.* Another wave of unease passed over him.

Now wide awake, he turned back and stared into the darkness. *What the hell could be wrong?*

"Everything…" he answered aloud.

"Hmm? You okay?" Sarah asked, her voice filled with sleep.

"Yes," he said, his voice strangely cold. "I'm fine, go back to sleep."

"Mmm… Lie down with me." She pulled open the tie at the top of her gown, took his hand in hers and held it between her breasts. "Hold me, love…"

"Sarah, I don't know…"

"Shhhh… Just hold me."

He looked at her; she lay in the moonlight with her eyes half-closed with sleep. Rest had been so spotty for him, it had been weeks since they had even lay together. *Blue eyes in the dawn. Beautiful…* He lay down slowly and she slid across the bed and put her head on his shoulder and an arm across his chest.

"Try to relax…"

As he lay beside her, she slid her hand around his waist and pulled herself to him. They kissed softly at first, and then more urgently, their hands moving slowly, knowingly, over each other. He slid her nightgown further up to her waist and looked at her; the moonlight coming in the window cast light blue shadows across her hips and in the soft dark wisps between. Daniel leaned over to kiss her neck and shoulders and breathed in her warmth, but his mind raced; the unease lingered. *Blue-white moonlight on pale skin reminds me...of what?* As they pulled each other close, Sarah lifted her hips and with a quiet moan, she reached down to guide him.

The vision came quite suddenly. *Dead faces... Fredericksburg.* He abruptly rolled over and sat up on the side of the bed. Sarah rose behind him.

"Daniel? Good Lord, what's wrong? What is it...?"

"Just leave me be, would you..." His body shook as the past swept over him.

A hard stab of cold brought him from the void. *Hard ground. Goddamn cold, hard ground...* He was lying face down and the chill rose through his body in waves. He tried to open his eyes and found the lids sticky with frost. He rolled over and brought a hand up to see if his eyes were fairly open, for he could see nothing. A deep, thick cough rose from his chest that bullied him conscious. Now, even numb with cold, the side of his head throbbed with a searing pain. He felt the scalp and found delicate ice crystals of matted blood over his left ear. *Wounded...again.* He slowly moved his arms and legs to check: the limbs felt like lead, but moved well enough, and the rest of his body seemed in one piece. He tried to collect his thoughts. *Where the hell am I...?* A humming sound rose and fell in the chill air all around: after listening for a moment, it became clear it was not one sound, but a mix of hundreds of low moans and other unrecognizable noises.

Spencer lifted himself on his elbows, and the pain in his head rose in response. Finally, his eyes adjusted and he gradually made out some detail: the icy ground dimly reflected the half moon above, creating a blue-white glow that lit the air around him. *Oh God...* Stretching off into the gloom, scores of dark bundles lay motionless in the stubble field around him; pale blue faces staring blankly to the sky, streaked with what looked to be black paint. *Not paint. Blood...* The landscape from a nightmare. *But where...?* He rubbed his eyes and recalled something someone – *Quinn* – taught him about getting one's bearings at night: *Stop thinking and just see the place with sunlight.* Seemed damned foolish when Quinn said it, but... *Old cornfield, long wooded ridge ahead... Fredericksburg.*

For some time he leaned on his arms, dazedly watching each shallow breath form a small cloud before him, floating indecisive the air, until it abandoned the effort and disappeared. *Nothingness...* A voice rose in the back of his mind. *Move. You need to move or you'll die...* The side of his head threatened to burst at the effort, but slowly he moved to his hands and knees.

Across the field, dim lights bobbed in the distance, moving this way and back. No explanation seemed to fit – perhaps the lost souls of those that lay torn around him? *No. Lanterns...* Stretcher-bearers looking for wounded, but which army are they? *Does it make any difference? Move – now...* The metal stock plate of a rifle gleamed a foot or so away; he grabbed the barrel, stood the gun upright and used it as a prop to climb to his feet. As he stood, the night whirled around him and he gagged. When his insides settled, he took a long pull from his canteen; the icy water soothed the throat, but made his scalp throb all the more.

Hobbling on the rifle, Spencer haltingly made his way across the uneven ground. After several minutes' effort, he knew he was making little headway: the lights remained far in the distance. *Keep moving...* He moved slowly, his mind still a jumble of unrelated thoughts, until he settled on one: the vista at home on a night like this, looking toward the frost-covered valley below. He started a smile, but the pleasant image didn't last; dark memories of the previous day took over, and spattered the vision like an early winter rain on window glass.

After the slaughter at Antietam, Lincoln replaced General McClellan with Ambrose Burnside, a general of large whiskers, but little confidence and less judgment. Spurred by the "On To Richmond" cries of the newspapers and a mild winter, Burnside decided to strike Lee's scattered army at Fredericksburg. A series of delays postponed the crossing of the Rappahannock River for three weeks, once again allowing Lee to reunite his army – and build a seven-mile long line of defenses on ridges west of Fredericksburg. On December 13, Burnside ordered a futile series of attacks against this line, losing 13,000 men in eight hours. The attack south of town was to cross a broad farm field that would come to be known as The Slaughter Pen.

December 13, 1862: Morning
Fredericksburg, Virginia

Blam-hmm! The crash of nearby cannon heaved the lieutenant from sleep. With a groan, he rolled out of the blanket and leaned up on his elbows to look around; as he did so, his arms sank with a *crr-issh* into the half-frozen mud below him. *Dammit...* A heavy cough rose in his chest, joining the cacophony of others breaking the damp air. The wet Virginia winter had sickened just about everyone to some degree. In counterpoint to the staccato coughing, half a dozen cannon from a Maine battery thundered nearby, hurling destruction toward the fog-shrouded ridge to the west where the enemy lay hidden. Spencer watched the New Englanders toil over their pieces; several had shed their overcoats, and labored over the guns in their shirtsleeves. *Warm for December. Damn odd.* Despite the warm air, a chill breeze tugged at the banks of fog, gradually revealing muted browns of a late fall landscape that stood out but little from the dull gray sky above.

Blam-hmm! The half-frozen ground heaved in response, and the blasts rumbled down the valley like old thunder; Spencer's ribcage throbbed in reply. The wound from Antietam had healed somewhat, but the skin showed a dark purple welt and the ribs beneath still pained him. Blamm-mmm! Spencer cursed under his breath, shook his overcoat flaps back, and pulled himself out of the ooze as best he could. He stretched, and looked about as he scraped the caked reddish mud from his sleeves. The regiment lay in an open field of corn stubble; the other brigades of the division lay in long blue lines two or three hundred yards in front of them. Behind the regiment, a hedgerow-lined coach road led to the old colonial town of Fredericksburg that lay somewhere in the fog to the north. He pulled his watch from his vest: 10:17 a.m. *Again we wait...*

The day before, the thick mist had hidden their crossing of the Rappahannock. That morning, the brigade had moved from the river up to a farm a mile or so from the Rebel lines. There they received orders to halt, and there they still waited. The element of surprise, along with hopes to crush Lee's army, disappeared as no further word came. Between boredom and exhaustion, most of the men had immediately fallen asleep.

Not all that long before, Spencer would have grit his teeth and cursed at the lost opportunity and the lives it would cost; lately, a numb resignation had replaced his anger. He pulled the rubber blanket from his knapsack, spread it on the semi-frozen ground, and lay back. *We will be here until we lose enough men to fulfill orders.* He looked at his watch again, but did not note the time. *And we're waiting still... Death must be late.* Lieutenant Daniel Spencer would do the best by his men, but the hell with the goddamn generals, the reporters, and the politicians pounding their chests. *Let them get out here in this shit...*

He blew a sigh through his teeth and pulled his last letter from Sarah from his vest. She was expecting their first child and her words welled with anticipation. He unfolded it to the back page; *You know my love stays with you...* Lovely phrase, he thought, always ends her letters this way. He had no sooner refolded the page than he dozed off. He felt the vague spinning sensation as slipped toward sleep, his thoughts floating back to their home on the mountain...Sarah. *Blue eyes in the dawn... You know my love stays with you...*

Dah-doommm... Back across the Rappahannock, batteries of heavier field guns now roared in unison; Spencer opened his eyes and squinted up into the pale gray clouds as shells screeched overhead in long arcs that led toward the far ridge. Sergeant Quinn's wooly head appeared silhouetted in the sky over him.

"Those are them big damn twenty-pounders, L'tenit. I'd not want to be on the other end of that." Quinn gazed at the distant ridgeline and shook his head. "Poor Reb bastards... Wellsir, I think them Lancaster County boys up the line might have coffee – kin I get you some?"

"Coffee sounds good, Conall, see what you can do."

Quinn saluted and slogged off through the mud. Spencer stared off toward the far ridge; as quickly as the morning fog faded, it was replaced by thick, acrid smoke drifting over the river from the cannon. *Like Antietam. No. This is different...the Rebs aren't firing back.* Other than the one or two hidden cannon that pounded them earlier, the Southerners were strangely silent. *They're waiting for something...* He stared into the mist and bit his cheek. *Us...* He laid his face against his forearm and despite the din, dozed off again.

The sun shone dully at mid-sky when he started awake again; all hell was breaking loose across the fields to southwest. The brigade lines that had been in front of them were now far in advance across the field. As Spencer leaned up, he found a tin of luke-warm coffee beside him. *Good old Quinn.* Peering into the smoke that drifted across the stubble field, he could make out long ranks of blue cresting a rise of ground in the middle of the field, cheering with their customary *Huzzahh!* Abruptly, the cheers were drowned in the blast of gunfire from the woods beyond; the blue uniforms disappeared into the white cloud that rolled over the rise. Daniel dropped his head to his arm again. *And so it begins…*

The lieutenant sat up, gulped the tepid coffee and gazed at the shapes moving in the pale cloud: clumps of wounded men began to appear, making their way back through the corn stubble; blue couriers criss-crossed the broad field, threading their way amidst the injured. Behind the company line, Colonel McCoy stood quietly talking with officers from other regiments; despite a high fever, the colonel had returned to lead the Pennsylvanians, and now leaned against his horse, pale and soaked with sweat despite the cool air. A rider came toward them at full gallop, trailing a string of blue-coated aides. *That would be Gibbon...* John Gibbon was the new division commander; a regular army officer, hard by the book, and by the look of him, not pleased with how the day was going. *Won't be long now...*

Jim MacThompson walked over and knelt down. With McCoy's return to the regiment, it was with a certain relief that Spencer returned command of the company to MacThompson. The captain took off his leather gloves and pulled a handkerchief from his vest to wipe his face.

"Well," he said, "It's finally up and at 'em, Daniel. Word has it Meade's boys have got into the Rebel line in those woods up the hill. The rest of the division already pitched in; our brigade is next. Looking like the 107th will be the flank of the advance, so keep your eyes open. Let's get all our boys ready."

Sure enough, commands echoed from regiment to regiment, and mixed with the odd cacophony of groans, coughs, and clattering equipment as a thousand men rose to their feet. Spencer gazed down the ranks of his company; he thought back to the afternoon they left Harrisburg. *Let's get all our boys ready? Not that many left...and certainly not boys anymore.* The regiment came to attention, and the lieutenant took position just behind the line with Quinn just to his left. In this position, they were what the manual called "file-closers," charged with keeping the company in a tight line and firing straight. *File closers...we're trying to maintain order in hell.*

He bit at his cheek. *Until we have lost enough men...* Spencer looked at Quinn and the sergeant bobbed his head and winked. The customary quiet ribbing and remarks still ran down the line, but smiles and laughs gradually turned to a grim, set gaze toward the pale cloud of smoke that drifted across the field towards them.

Down the line, McCoy bellowed, "107th Pennsylvania! Forward at the quick step – March!"

The broad blue line lurched forward at a rapid walk across the ice-crusted mire. The brigade crested the rise in the middle of the field and smoke and noise rolled in to meet them. Cannon balls from the Southern artillery appeared out of the white smoke like welling ink spots taking dimension, and then bounded across the ground to plow into the ranks; bullets zipped from the chaos down the slope and found their mark. "Steady boys…close up."

Just over the rise, the regiment halted, coughing and breathless. Spencer sucked at the air; the earthy smell was gone, and burnt sulfur coated his throat. He wiped the cold sweat from his forehead with his sleeve and focused on the figures that appeared in the smoke just ahead: one of the regiments that advanced earlier, at least what remained of it, was reforming around their regimental flags. *God, they're already shot to pieces...* The officers moved about quickly, trying to restore order to the disorganized formation. The blast was more felt than heard.

While the lieutenant watched, a shell screamed in from the woods and exploded at the center of the mass of men. He cringed under the shock of the detonation, but he could not take his eyes off the nightmarish collage: the flags and those underneath disappeared amidst an orange flame that turned to ashen smoke and a slow spray of crimson. A smoldering piece of the regiment's banner flew into the air, fluttering to the ground with a faint trail of smoke in its wake; just behind the line, an officer spun like a top and crashed to the ground. Beneath the slowly thinning cloud, several forms lay unmoving, thrown into the mud; others sat up, staring blankly, patting various body parts to see if the gore that covered them was their own. Nearby, Quinn's hoarse, but firm voice bellowed, "Steady fellows. Stay in line."

Something on the ground caught Spencer's eye: almost unrecognizable, the section of flag tossed from the explosion lay at his feet: wisps of smoke rose from where red and white ribbed cloth still burned; the remnant untouched by the flame was soaked with blood. He felt his fingernails dig into his palms. Then, through the uproar, he thought he heard a whispered, *Daniel...* He shifted his gaze down to his hands and unclenched them; they were coated with a dried reddish mud – and shaking uncontrollably. *Steady...* He closed his eyes for a moment and ground his teeth.

The remainder of the forward line fell back around the Pennsylvanians. Sergeant Quinn had appeared at his side, his whiskered face flushed and steaming in the cool air. "Poor bastards!" He peered sidelong at the lieutenant, and cupped his hand to be heard.

"'L'tenit? You're alright, sir?"

Spencer, still gazing at his hands, remembered himself; he cleared his throat as he straightened up, and looked at Quinn. "Yes, I'm fine. How are we doing?"

"Wellsir," Quinn yelled hoarsely, "Our man Murphy is wounded in the shoulder and gone to the rear. Otherwise, so far, so good. Cap'n Deegan of Company C got hit pretty bad, looks to lose most of a leg." Quinn nodded his head behind them. "And it looks like we're moving forward again sir..."

Just yards away, General Gibbon and the Colonel were talking; their nervous mounts turned in tight circles about each other as the officers shouted back and forth to be heard amidst the roar. The colonel nodded, drew a quick salute to Gibbon, and rode over to MacThompson at the end of the regiment's line.

Again came the whisper. *Daniel...*

Spencer shook his head to clear it and blew a breath through his teeth. He squinted back at Captain MacThompson, who was trying to make himself understood: "Fix-x-x, Bayonet!" Hoarse commands followed, bellowed down the line as the order spread from company to company. Almost as one, the entire regiment lowered their rifles, whipped the long triangular blades from their sheaths and snapped them onto the barrels. The front rank dropped their rifles forward at hip level with a shout. Spencer turned to the sergeant and yelled. "Well, Sergeant, now or never. You ready?" Quinn, his jaw set, nodded.

"Forward at the double-quick! Charge!" The colonel's final words were almost lost in the swirl of noise, but when the color guard stepped forward with the flags, the whole regiment followed in a shallow V, surging down the slope with a hoarse, "Huzz-aahhh!"

Through the haze ahead, the Rebel battle-line was just visible, sheltered behind a low railroad bank that paralleled the edge of the woods. Some of the gray figures were retreating by ones and twos, but the balance of the Southern ranks held, and firing another volley, disappeared in a bank of ashen smoke. The lieutenant jogged down the slope, his rasping breaths melded with the cheers, the zip of lead through the thick air, the crashing thud of men and equipment hitting the cold earth.

Reaching the near side of the embankment, the charge lost momentum as many dove against the bank for cover, sucking in the acrid air, while flashes burst over their heads from the Rebel barrels just yards away. Spencer's mind raced. Despite the chaos, the world around him seemed to have fallen still. *Until we have lost enough men... We can't just stay here. Do something!*

He unsheathed his sword and waved it over his head. He heard his voice yelling. "Give 'em hell!" He scrambled up the embankment, onto the tracks, and stood up. The roar now grew around him and the rest of the regiment surged past him like a wave. As the blue line rose into view, the tree line in front of them exploded with rifle-fire. The blast again shattered the momentum. Spencer lowered his sword and glared into the haze. *Men are dying all around me, but still I live. Now. Here I am. Kill me now...* In the midst of the bedlam, Quinn appeared and grabbed his arm.

"Can't have you gettin' too impatient, L'tenit!" He pulled Spencer down, tumbling them into the low ground beyond the bank.

As the dirty gray cloud billowed overhead, the lieutenant lifted himself to his hands and knees from the pile of bodies that lay at the foot of the embankment; he rose to one knee, unconsciously wiping the gore from his hands as he gazed about. *I've gotten us shot all to hell again...*

He shook his head again to clear the numb roar and looked about; a few feet away, Quinn had gathered several of the company; they knelt in the muddy ground, gulping at the thick air. The rest of the regiment was nowhere to be seen, but down the smoke-shrouded gully, Spencer could see the flashes from Rebel rifles still firing over the tracks. *We've flanked them. And they don't see us...* He grabbed Quinn and pointed toward the dim gray figures in the smoke. The sergeant understood immediately. Without a sound, the two men grabbed blue-coated arms and shoulders and managed to form a ragged line facing toward the Southerners. Quinn nodded at Spencer.

The lieutenant again waved his sword above his head and screamed above the din: "Fire! Fire at will!" The company fired a ragged volley, and several of the gray figures toppled onto the bank or fell back into the ditch; others fled for the woods.

"At's showing 'em, L'tenit!" Quinn yelled hoarsely, and grinning, held his fist in the air.

Spencer nodded in reply and turned back toward the wooded hill beyond the railroad. Then it came again: he felt that strange pause: the barely felt breeze shifting direction. The day had turned; blue figures were running through the smoke in the trees ahead, running toward him; running for their lives. In an instant, a series of shell bursts shattered the tops of the barren trees above them. His last image was of a large limb hurtling towards him.

Daniel...

The dull ache in his temples remained as the whisper faded. Everything was still blue-dark and his body was numb with cold. The warmth grew around him and arms held him tightly.

Sarah said quietly, "It's alright, love. I'm here."

Home... Still sitting on the edge of the bed, he turned and looked at Sarah, who leaned back and looked at him anxiously.

"Please say something. What's happening?"

"Just let me be, will you...?"

He stood slowly and stretched, twisting his head trying to unclench his neck muscles. He turned to look at Sarah; she had leaned back in the dim light, her hands dropped helplessly to her lap.

"Sorry. I didn't mean that, Sarah. I'm sorry. Just give me a moment..."

"It happened again: you dreamt you were there, didn't you? I'm worried about you. Please. What can I do?"

"I'm just exhausted. I need to get some sleep..."

As he lay back, she studied him for a moment and then pulled the coverlet over them. She lay down and curled up beside him. As he lay clearing his head, Daniel could feel her watching him in the dim light. He turned toward her.

"It will be alright, Sarah. Go to sleep."

"Daniel," she whispered, "please just remember: all that is over. You're home now. I am with you. And we will get through this."

She sighed, still watching him. Soon though, her eyes grew heavy and closed, her breathing slowed as she dozed off. He lay beside her, his eyes open and gazing out the window. Much of the sky now showed a dark blue; moonlight glowed around the edges of the scuttering clouds. *Yes, but I am not home, and it's not over...*

July 5, 1863: Morning
South Mountain, Pennsylvania

Dawn's thick gray overcast broke the night's promise of better weather. Large raindrops patted at the bedroom window where Spencer stood. Once more shrouded in fog, the valley below showed little to focus on; he watched nonetheless.

Sarah had risen early. In the wake of the night's troubled dreams, she left Daniel to sleep, and passed the morning cleaning and making work. It was now almost mid-morning and she pulled a chair to the window to relax, gazing at the yard in the rain. The wind blew strong from the east, spattering the rain in small streams against the outside of the window. The view of the yard blurred where the water ran at the window's edge, so Sarah barely noticed the black shape move into view. She leaned forward to see more clearly: a large black horse – the Rebel officer's mare. She jumped to her feet, and sent the chair to the floor with a crash.

"Daniel!"

Even as she cried out, Spencer was already bounding down the stairs. He ran to the window: other than the mare, the yard was empty; there was no sign of the Southern officer, but his saddle lay sideways on the horse's flank. Daniel blew a sigh through his lips, and sat down while he pulled on his boots.

"Wait..." Her face pale and terrified, Sarah grabbed his arm with one hand and placed the other hand against his chest. "What if there's more Rebels this time? You don't know what they might do..."

He lifted his arm from her grasp, but checked his irritation. "Sarah, let go dammit. I'm fine. And I think I have pretty good idea what Rebs will do, but I don't see anything more than a horse. Do you?"

Her protests were getting nowhere. Sarah stepped back and wrung her hands, alternately looking out the window at the mare, then back to Daniel as he put on his hat and coat. She reached for the shotgun that lay on the mantel, "Well, at least take the damn gun!"

He stopped, taken aback by her outburst, and turned to see her holding out the scattergun. *Calm down...*

"Sarah...it's fine, I'll be the soul of caution. That's the Rebel major's horse. I don't see any other Rebs, and if there are, one gun is not going to help. Look at that saddle – it's not looking like the man chose to dismount. He was in bad shape; alive or no, he can't be far. I at least need to look for him. Don't worry, I'll be right back."

Outside, the yard was awash with rainwater. Daniel pulled the brim of his hat down, folded his arms against the downpour, and leaping the deeper puddles, walked slowly toward the trough. The Rebel's horse watched him approach and backed away with a weak snort. Daniel stopped, moved where the horse could see him clearly, then held his hands out and kept his eyes lowered. He spoke quietly. "Shhh. It's okay girl; remember me?" The mare blew as he reached out and stroked her neck, but steadied as he spoke. "Shhhh. You've had a long night. Let's get you out of the rain." He slowly picked up the fallen reins, and led the horse into the barn.

He looked the animal over; other than needing food and rest, the big mare looked in fair shape. But the already raw skin of the animal's back showed a shallow welt where the loose cinch had scored it when the saddle turned; the belts that had once held the Rebel in the saddle were broken and dragged on the barn floor. He picked up the torn ends of wet leather. *Didn't last long...* He carefully uncinched the saddle and led the horse to the stall next to Tobey. The mare blew and shivered some as Daniel dabbed salve over her back, but she remained calm. He filled the hay manger with timothy, and the horse ate eagerly. Tobey turned and nickered at him quietly.

"You're in better shape than she is, old man," Daniel said, "Don't be so greedy."

Daniel left both animals to feed and walked out into the rain. Latching the barn door, he gazed down the lane where he had last seen the Southerner. *He couldn't have gotten far before he died...* He walked down the road, keeping to the rise in the center; to each side, courses of rainwater sought their way downhill in the wide troughs created by the passage of countless wagon wheels. Ahead, the lane skirted their cornfield and entered a grove of old oaks, where the path narrowed and eventually met the road that led into the valley.

At the edge of the grove stood an ancient tree, its massive trunk gainsaid the thin lower limbs bent with age and spare of leaves; beneath it lay the Rebel officer. He remembered: *a lifeless gray uniform in the tall grass...some mother's son.* "Not again," Daniel said aloud. "Not this time..." Half-expecting the body to be cold and stiff with rigor, he knelt down and turned the Rebel over. Instead, the man groaned and twitched as raindrops hit his eyelids. *One tough son of a bitch... Help him.*

"Major, Can you hear me?"

The Southerner muttered to himself at first, but then came a whispered, "Yes..." Daniel found his canteen in the grass beside him. *Still half full.* He knelt over the man and lifted his head. The Rebel drank eagerly, and gagged for his haste.

"You may well be one tough Reb, but go slow now."

The man seemed to gain some strength as he drank. His lips moved in a half-whisper, "Obliged, sir. Thank you." He narrowed his eyes and studied Daniel.

"I know you..."

"Yes. Name's Spencer. You were at my farm yesterday for water."

"You gave me food...those biscuits..." The Rebel gazed about and spoke, his voice a little stronger. "My horse... Have you seen my mare? I need the mare...trying to get home."

Home. Daniel frowned at the irony. Another man trying to get home... He eyed the bloody bandage on the Rebel's thigh. *Not many ways he's getting far with that wound...*

"Major. Yes, I found your mare; she's up in my barn, but you didn't get far the last time you tried riding. You don't have lots of choices here. You can't get home right now. You're going to need some care, so I'm going to carry you back to my farm. Probably going to hurt like hell too."

He put the major's hat low over his face to keep the rain off, cradled the man in his arms, and staggered upright. Both men groaned at the effort. Daniel turned and moved haltingly up the path through the rain. The old wound in his side now ached at the load, and as the incline grew, his legs burned with each step. Stopping to catch his breath, he shifted the weight of the major's body; the Rebel shuddered with the movement, but stifled the groan.

The rain had slowed, but still dripped off Spencer's forehead, blurring his vision, and ran off his nose where he blew at the drops. The rebel major gasped and clutched at his coat front.

"Sir, please...just need my horse. My home is just across the river."

"At this rate, major, neither of us may make it."

At the top of the lane, Daniel stopped again, exhausted, leaning against the planked side of the barn; Sarah was already running from the house.

"Oh my God, Daniel. He's alive? Here, let me help you get him into the house."

"No...no further...the barn. Open the door..."

Sarah ran around to the barn entrance and swung the doors open; she looked around the interior quickly, pulled an old blanket from the shelf and laid it in the hay of the spare stall. With the last of his strength, Daniel staggered through the door out of the rain. Sarah helped him lower the Rebel, each taking an arm and laying him back onto the blanket. Unable to swallow any more pain, the man groaned piteously. Daniel dropped to his knees beside the Southerner, gasping for air. Sarah grabbed his shoulders.

"Daniel, are you alright?"

His ribcage throbbed with each breath drawn, but he nodded and waved her off. "Fine, fine... Just need...catch a breath."

Spencer sat up, holding his side with one arm, and managed a wan smile; Sarah slowly let him go and turned to the Rebel. She studied the officer, scowling at the gray uniform, but then slowly reached out, pushed the hair from the man's forehead and held her hand to his pale brow.

"He has a high fever."

The officer opened his eyes and looked at her, his expression filled with agony. Sarah's eyes softened for a moment, but she lifted her head and turned away, her lips compressed. She cleared her throat and turned to Daniel. "I'll see what I can do."

Sarah stood, looking down at the Rebel; she wiped her hands on her apron, and walked quickly to the house. Some minutes later, she returned, a second blanket folded over her arm. She spread the blanket over the Rebel and knelt beside him, her face lined with scorn.

"For all the harm you people have caused us," she said under her breath, "I should just let you lay. But I can't do that."

She reached down into her apron and pulled out a bottle of amber liquid and a large spoon. "Here, you need to swallow some of this. It's laudanum. It will cut the pain." She filled the spoon, lifted the officer's head and slowly poured it into his mouth. He gagged at first, but took the liquid and lay back with a sigh. Sarah watched the Rebel for a moment: he still shivered, but his pain seemed to ease.

Daniel stood and walked to where Sarah was kneeling. She rose to face him, her face still set with disapproval. He took her hands in his and spoke quietly. "He's not the enemy now, Sarah, he's a wounded man."

She lifted her arms away from Daniel's hold, gave him a prickly glance. "Really. After all that has happened, I don't know how you can say that." She realized her hair had fallen and lay wet on her shoulders; she pulled it to the back of her neck and composed herself. "But I'm a Christian woman; I'll do what I can for him." She looked back to the Southerner. "He is chilled to the bone. The rain looks to have stopped; should we carry him to the house?"

Daniel studied the man's face. "Looks to have lost a lot of blood. I don't know what's kept him alive this long; moving him this far just about did him in. I think we best keep him here for the time being. I'll get the stove going, maybe get some of my old clothes – getting rid of that wet uniform will help. And we're going to need to change that bandage."

Sarah turned and returned to the house to collect dry clothing and linen to dress the wound; Spencer set about coaxing the ancient stove back to life. As the flames kindled, he studied this enemy who now lay helpless in his barn. *Now he's just another soldier trying to get home...* At one time, the man might have stood a bit taller and broader, but now some of Daniel's clothes would make do. He knelt next to the Rebel.

The major opened his eyes, squinting as if looking from afar. He spoke quietly, "What is today?"

He had to think. "Sunday... Sunday the fifth."

The major stared off, trying to focus on the missing time. He whispered, "I was wounded on...Wednesday. July first. They took my limb that night. As I recall, wasn't much left worth keeping..."

"What is your name, Major?"

The laudanum had done its work. "Stanton," he said distantly, "Major John Stanton..."

"Well, Major Stanton, I know you want to get home; I'm afraid you can't go far right now though. And we're going to have to move you some to get you into dry clothes; and then get the old dressing off your leg. Think you can bear all that?"

The Rebel looked at him blurrily and nodded. "God willing, sir," he rasped, "Perhaps...just more Yankee biscuits might help..."

Spencer tilted his head back and laughed aloud. "Yes," he said, "I'll bet they would at that, Major, I'll bet they would." The Southerner began a smile, but then grimaced again and slipped into unconsciousness.

By midday, they had done all they could to make the Southerner comfortable. Sarah's mood had softened, and she sat beside Daniel on a milking stool with elbows on her knees, pushing her damp hair back over her temples. She stood up.

"We should let him sleep," she whispered.

"You go on, Sarah, I'll stay here awhile yet."

"I will wait with you then."

"Sarah..."

"I will wait with you." She looked at him with that slight, determined smile and resumed her seat.

Daniel sat back in the hay, drew his legs up in front of him and watched the Southerner's labored breathing. He put his head on his arms and tried to relax. Suddenly, the rumble of cannon rolled up the hillside. Daniel started, lifted his head and listened carefully. Sarah stood quickly and looked to him with concern. More blasts, and not far away.

The major had awakened as well. The man's face was ashen, but his eyes were clear and focused. He leaned up as much as he could.

"Artillery. Where is it?"

"Please lay back, Major. They're down the valley to the south. Sounds like around Fairfield."

The Rebel thought for a moment. "Yes…we would have to pass that way. Rearguard maybe…" He smiled weakly, "Guess we aren't leaving…without a fight."

Sarah looked from Daniel to the Rebel. "So it's over? Lee is retreating?"

"Retreating…" The major thought on it, "Can't say. Few days ago, we had your boys on the run. Next I hear, we're pulling out. But over? No. You Yanks best be careful. General Lee may have taken a licking, but it's not over."

Whatever the outcome, the rumble of the guns soon faded. The Southerner sighed; if he had further opinion, he kept his thoughts to himself and dozed off again. The war would go on without him. Minutes later, he reawakened. "Mister…Spencer?"

"Rest, Major."

"I am…indebted to you." The Rebel's breath seemed labored. "But I would ask one more thing of you now. There is a letter from my wife in the wallet on my saddle; would you get it for me?"

Daniel nodded. He lit an oil lamp, retrieved the saddlebags, and knelt beside the major. As he opened the flap, the inside smelled of the wet leather and gun oil; inside was a wallet showing some bills and a stained envelope folded inside. He handed it to Stanton, who gingerly removed the pages from the envelope as if opening something priceless. He held the letter up to the lamp, his hand wavering, but squinting and turning it back and forth to read the fine script. The pages trembled in his hand as a leaf about to fall.

"I am afraid my vision isn't what it should be. Mrs. Spencer, I understand your...feelings toward me, but if I could trouble you to read this for me, it would be a great comfort."

Sarah started. She looked to Daniel with her mouth open slightly as if to object, but then dropped her gaze and replied, "Of course, major." She held the letter to the light and started to read, then stopped and looked at the Southerner.

"Major, this is between you and your wife..."

"M'am...I have little need of privacy now. It would be a great comfort if you would continue."

Sarah began to read, uncomfortably at first, but then with a familiarity as though the words were of her own making. The first paragraphs spoke of the man's family, their farm in Northern Virginia, of his wife's difficulties managing without him. But as she read, the words became those only shared between a man and his wife. As she continued, Daniel listened uncomfortably, as if eavesdropping on a conversation that was not his to hear.

Last instant you wrote with concern that after so long, the memory of you might fade from our son's heart. You need not worry so: until you come home my love, know we are with you, and you with us. As sure as the morning's sun shines still, whether warming our porch as it is now, or hidden by clouds but warming the spring rain, know you are in our hearts always.

You wrote that you have changed, that the war has scarred you, that the man who left our home is not the one whose return I so look for. If as you say, all your trials have sorely worn at you, that you can never hope to find any good in this world again, I would remind my husband that although everything fine and good seems ruined, that which is most precious is not this world of conflict and sorrow, but what lives on in our hearts. Please believe me love. I will prove this to you in a thousand ways when next we meet. Please come home to us as soon as you can. Until then I look to your return and our days ahead together.

Your loving wife,

Elizabeth

The letter's last words caught in Sarah's throat. She stared at the pages and sobbed. She looked up at the Southerner.

"That is lovely, Major. Your wife must be…" She stopped and held her breath.

Daniel gazed into the flame of the oil lamp. *That which is most precious is not this world of conflict and sorrow, but what lives on in our hearts…* He felt Sarah pull on his forearm; he leaned forward and looked closely at the major. Unlike minutes before, when the man's face was strained with agony, his expression was now calm, and his gaze fixed in the distance. Daniel reached forward and closed the man's eyes. *He's home...*

By late afternoon, much of the storm had blown to the east; as the sun lowered behind the mountain, the tall thunderheads turned a rose color. Sarah sat quietly on the front steps, her feelings a conflict; the man lying in the barn had been their enemy; another time, it would have been his place to kill her husband. On this afternoon, however, he was another soul whose family would wait in vain. As she thought, her gaze drifted back and forth, from the mist-filled valley, then to the yard to where Daniel was working; he had labored a good part of the afternoon, trimming planks milled to repair the carriage shed into a coffin. She first thought the effort excessive. *I'll not see another good man just laid in the dirt*, Daniel had said. She watched in silence as he measured another board to fit the lid.

Before long, they hitched the mare to the log sled, and drew the Southerner's coffin down the lane to bury him near the edge of the grove where Daniel found him that morning. When the couple had finished turning the soft wet earth onto the Rebel's grave, they stood quietly for a moment.

Sarah turned to Daniel and took his hand. "I feel badly for some of those things I said; I feel what I feel. But I would like to find this man's family and let them know where he's buried. Could we do that?"

He looked at her with some surprise; he nodded, "Of course. I'm sure there's an address on that letter. I'll finish up here, why don't you go on ahead; I'll be up in a minute."

Sarah nodded and walked slowly up the lane. Daniel smoothed the mound of earth over the grave and placed the shovel and pick on the sled; he sat at the base of the large oak to rest for a moment. He drew his knees up, and leaned his head back against the cool bark. *That which is most precious is not this world of conflict and sorrow, but what lives on in our hearts...* In the fading light, the mountain air was cooling quickly, and the mist below had started to clear. The gunfire had ended hours before, and the darkening valley before him was quiet.

His thoughts turned over the afternoon. How different was this man and his family – this enemy? He sensed an answer, but it was just out of his reach. *Trying to get home; just another warrior done with war. And me? Home, but the war is not done with me. Is there no forgetting...?* A slight breeze blew the lush green smell of wet corn across the slope. The image was quite fresh: *Bright green leaves, dark red blood...Antietam.* The feeling of dread rose in his chest, the lingering dark memory; but this time, it was just that. He leaned his head on his arms and unbidden tears fell onto the ground below.

The Northern attacks against Lee's trenches at Fredericksburg were a horrid failure; the Federals quietly retreated and pulled up the bridges behind them, leaving behind over a thousand of their comrades in shallow graves. The Confederates promptly reoccupied the now ravaged town and the stalemate began anew. On the east side of the Rappahannock, the Federal army again lay in camp while the senior officers pondered their next move. Nearby, the town of Falmouth became one enormous hospital.

January 7, 1863: Early Morning
Falmouth, Virginia

The embers of the woodfire sparked and flared where he absent-mindedly poked at them with a bent ramrod; otherwise, there was little to indicate he had any interest in his surroundings. The daytime temperatures of the Virginia winter had been oddly mild. Even so, the smell of hickory smoke mixed with the ropes of evergreen that draped the neat rows of hospital tents might have reminded a visitor of holidays past up north – were it not for the moans rising from inside the pale canvas walls. Even so, the sweet aroma briefly stirred his memory. *Holidays...home. You know my love stays with you...* Yet the thought stirred no feeling.

Spencer leaned back in an old chair in front of his tent, legs stretched in front of him. Bandages wrapped the injuries to his neck and the side of his head. From the pieces of bark and splinters pulled from the wound, the doctors guessed he had collided violently with a tree, but could not begin to imagine how. He himself remembered little of the injury. It mattered little to him one way or another; at this rate, soon enough he would be nothing but scars. *Yet I survive when so many others do not...*

Despite the optimism of the doctors who said the wounds were healing, the blinding headaches and hacking cough that developed since showed little sign of improvement; his demeanor even less so. *I have had enough...*

With the brigade camped just down the road, Spencer was fortunate enough to have frequent visitors, and Sergeant Quinn had been up almost daily. Their conversations were generally one-sided: Quinn talked about everything and nothing; Spencer sat quietly. Gradually, some of the story became clear: the regiment had made a stand at the railroad but was eventually overwhelmed; in the last, Quinn had returned that night to find the lieutenant hobbling across the field in a daze, and brought him to a hospital across the Rappahannock.

The previous day, Captain MacThompson had made a more pointed visit. Earlier that morning, the dull pain behind his eyes had driven Spencer to his cot, where he lay facing the canvas wall of the tent. He was dozing when he heard MacThompson's voice.

"You awake, Lieutenant?"

He turned over and started to rise to salute, but MacThompson waved him down and walked over to shake his hand. Spencer noted he now wore the straps of a lieutenant colonel.

"I hear from Sergeant Quinn you're coming along. How are you feeling, Dan?"

"Tolerable Capt... Sorry – Colonel."

MacThompson smiled, "I won't keep you Dan, but I have some news for you – good news. I know you've had one hell of a go of it. Quinn said you weren't altogether sure what happened back at that railroad." MacThompson pulled a chair next to the cot and sat down.

"I can tell you this: we made one of the few breakthroughs that afternoon, much of it thanks to you and your company. It did not go unnoticed; you've done well, and Colonel McCoy and I put you in for promotion: Captain of Company B. You've more than earned it."

Spencer felt some surprise, but could muster little enthusiasm for the conversation. He sighed, and said under his breath, "I see. Lost enough men to get a promotion... "

The colonel sat up and looked at him with uncertainty. He cleared his throat. "Excuse me...?"

"If I may speak freely Colonel? No. I don't remember much of what happened; but what seems clear to me is that no matter what we accomplished, it came to nothing. Again. We're back on this side of the river. Again. Whether it was no reinforcements, botched orders, or some other goddamn thing – what did we gain? Nothing. Every time we move a foot, we slide back three. Sure, soon enough another general will come in with another plan: we'll march off and find another field to kill and be killed, but we get nowhere. Nowhere. Colonel, don't you see? Even when I *do well*, more men die. I've become just another link in this chain of madness. I have had enough."

MacThompson stared and shook his head. "Dan. Look, I have been at this a while; every officer goes through what you feel. And it's normal to feel used up after the wounds you've taken. But you'll find your way; you just need some time..."

"You don't understand, Colonel. I'm finished."

"I'm sorry you feel that way." He frowned, and leaned forward, "Alright, then, Lieuten...excuse me, *Captain* Spencer. I am ordering you to give yourself a week. I can't see the army moving any time before then. Get some rest. Heal up. Then, if your mind is still made up, submit your resignation. I'll approve it and forward it on."

MacThompson looked at him for a moment. He stood, shaking his head again, and said quietly, "Don't get up. Get some rest, Captain Spencer." The colonel saluted, turned and left the tent quickly before Spencer could return the salute.

So, on this afternoon, the captain leaned forward, poking at the coals of the fire, turning the MacThompson's words over in his mind again. *Get some rest. Heal up.* Rest? His feelings since the battle had been but two: emptiness and rage; rage at what had happened to his life, emptiness because it was easier than the other. Neither emotion left him particularly rested. *What did he say? Wait one week more? Why? Is there a cure for feeling nothing?* He stared off into the embers, and a chill, damp gust blew in from the river.

"The great and auspicious moment has arrived to strike a great and mortal blow to the rebellion, and to gain that decisive victory which is due to the country,"
  – Maj. Gen. Ambrose Burnside, January 20, 1863.

In the month since Fredericksburg, morale had improved somewhat; General Burnside had regained a measure of credibility, at least with some in the ranks. Either way, the weather had been unseasonably clear and called for action on the part of the Federals. The orders came on January 20th: the First Corps was to march west, join the large force crossing at Banks Ford to outflank Lee's position on the Rappahannock. For several hours, their march went well. Then it started to rain.

January 21, 1863: Evening
North of Falmouth, VA

The storm all but smothered the Virginia countryside. As daylight started to fade, hundreds of men in blue huddled anonymously beside the flooded roadbed that led toward Warrenton; some collected under tent halves or tall bushes, others simply shivered in the icy rain, glad only to be out of the mud. With no discernable insignia, the captain sat among them. His thoughts drifted over the change wrought in just the past day; as no one thing stood out in importance, the memories came just as randomly. *But none of it makes one damn bit of difference...*

Despite his misgivings, after two weeks in the hospital, Spencer had felt well enough – and as company captain, obligated enough – to rejoin the regiment. Perhaps as MacThompson had said, the dark moods were only temporary; Spencer was finding they were not.

The orders arrived the day after the captain returned to camp: once again, the Army was moving to attack Lee's flank up the Rappahannock River. After a promising march of several miles, the regiment went into camp for the night. The rain started pattering on the tent flaps just after dark.

By dawn the next morning, the roads leading to the river crossings were awash. At mid-day, artillery and wagons were sinking axle-deep; not long after, worn-out horses and mules collapsed in their traces, half buried in the orange mud. Entire regiments were pulled from the march to help drag mired cannon. What little progress the men made came at a high cost: unable to move more than inches at a time, their resolve fell by the wayside as well. The thick slurry sucked the shoes from their feet, and within a few steps, the roadbed stone floating in the icy dirt sliced into the raw skin; thousands of bloody footprints froze into in the brown slush. By mid-afternoon, the Army was at a standstill.

Since that morning, Spencer had pulled his exhausted horse through the mire that lay foot-deep along the Warrenton Road. Each piece of hazy landscape that appeared dimly through the rain seemed tentative, as if depending solely on his slow progress through the mud. Before long, the horse slid into a sinkhole; despite Spencer's best efforts, the exhausted animal simply gave up: it its eyes rolled white, it slowly collapsed into the cold water and drowned. Dropping the limp reins in the mud, the captain half thought to lay down with the animal. *Not a bad way to die.* But Spencer kept moving – he tried to remember how far. *Half a mile? Or only a few yards?*

When he looked up, he was uncertain whether the brigade had passed him by, or was still somewhere in the murk behind. He found a rise of ground by the roadside and sat down heavily; he had nothing left. Despite the cold rain, the crimson welt from Antietam burned under his soaked uniform; his cold had worsened, and with each cough, his head pounded. The pain shrouded his thoughts, supplanted now by an even deeper sense of futility. *Every mother's son will get too used up some day...* If the battle for Fredericksburg had been a macabre tragedy, this maneuver belonged to the absurd. *Just sit... Nothing you've done made a difference; now you can barely move. There is nothing more any of us can do. Enough. No more...*

He had no idea how much time had passed when he heard the sergeant's voice bellowing in the distance.

"Cap-tain! Cap'n Spencer?"

Up the road slogged Quinn, squinting under the brim of his cap at the figures huddled on each side. He stopped in front of Spencer, peering across the road through the downpour. "Cap'n?" He waded over and shook Spencer's shoulder.

"Cap'n?" The sergeant now leaned over him, rain rolling off the brim of his kepi, his face steaming in the cold rain.

He gazed dully at Quinn, and the thought rang in his head: *I have nothing left. Leave me. No more...* But no words came.

"Come on, Cap'n. Let's get you back to camp. We best get goin' before we have ta swim. Can you walk, sir? It's not too far. Let's give it a go."

Quinn slid an arm under Spencer's, lifted him to his feet, and half-dragged him to the muddy road. With the sergeant's help, Spencer staggered along, at each step his head throbbing with pain, and he fell repeatedly in the mire. *Leave me. I have nothing left. No more...* Each time Quinn hefted him back to his feet.

As the old Warrenton Road neared Falmouth, army wagons crowded the path; beside the roadbed, teamsters had set lanterns to light the way in the murk. In the flickering half-light, a kaleidoscope of images past and present passed before Spencer's eyes: flashes of lightning the night before Antietam, the glittering lanterns in the cold chill of Fredericksburg, bright glimpses of clear sky amidst bloody corn stalks, all mixed with the long wavering shadows of draft animals straining in their harnesses. In the midst of all, Quinn's face appeared beside him in the dim light, humming one Irish tune or another, trying to keep Spencer awake and moving.

The next image Spencer clearly understood was the cold predawn of another hospital. A single candle came into focus, burning low in the damp air. In the wavering light, he made out overhead beams of a large wooden structure. The place smelled of camphor and mildewed clothing; rasping snores and low moans came from the dark around him. But the images were dull: the thoughts came slowly. He coughed weakly, and his chest ached, but his body seemed oddly distant. He remembered the feeling. *Laudanum. Another hospital... I'm still alive? Why? Nothing left. No more...* He slipped back into a black void.

July 6, 1863: Morning
South Mountain, Pennsylvania

The thought came just before the first glow of morning; for the rested, a time of clarity of thought; for the restless, a time of apprehension. *It's time...* What had happened at Gettysburg was a matter of concern for Sarah's family, but had risen as a dark question in Daniel's mind. *I need to know what happened. It's time.*

He leaned on the washstand and yawned. After burying the Southerner the evening before, the couple had a late supper. Sarah and he had eaten silently, each trying to understand how the death of this enemy – this man – had affected them so. Then they went to bed early, worn out from the day; but they made love long into the night. *Blue eyes in the dawn...*

Through the eastern window, the sun rose in a blaze of red below a dark gray cloud, long deep amber beams stretching across the shadowed valley below. He wondered at the contradiction: he had turned his back on the killing fields, but couldn't help but return to them.

Part of him said, I don't need to see that again...

The rest disagreed. Yes, you do. You should have been there...

He leaned over, cupping cool water from the washbasin in his hands, and held it to his face. *I should have...* He looked up at the mirror. *And then there's Rebecca.*

Sarah came up from behind him and reached out to caress his neck, but stopped short. "Did you say something?"

He looked at her image in the mirror. *Did I?* He cleared his throat.

"It's time I go."

"You mean to find Rebecca?"

He stared into the mirror. "Well...yes, it's time."

"Daniel, I thought we agreed to wait? Yes, my parents are worried about Becky; I'm worried about Becky. But you said yourself, she's probably safe. You don't know where the Rebels are; there was just gunfire in the valley yesterday. And," she paused, "You're not well."

"I'm as fine as I'm going to be. And I'm not only going there to find your sister. There is something I must do for myself: I need to know what happened there."

She stared at his reflection. "What happened? You know what happened: the Rebels are retreating..."

"No. You won't understand. I need to know more; what happened to my regiment. I should have been there; maybe it would have made a difference. I think this is what has been eating at me. I need to know."

"You're right, I don't understand. You've already done your part. Lord knows it almost killed you. Daniel..." She saw the determined reflection in the mirror. She stopped and lifted her chin, her expression adamant as well. "Fine," she said. "Then I will go with you. Rebecca is my sister..."

"Sarah, no. Please don't make this any harder."

"No. I'm going with you."

"Is this because of your sister? Do you think there's still something there..."

She turned and moved to the window. She gazed silently into the valley for a moment, and turned back to him, her eyes their deep blue.

"I won't say that didn't cross my mind. But, no, you said that was over long ago. I trust you both." She gazed back out the window.

"It's this," she said quietly, "If anything happens to you, I will have nothing left here anymore..."

He felt his throat thicken; he put his arms around her and pulled her close. "Sarah. Please, it's not safe for you." He leaned back and placed his hands on either side of her face. "But I won't leave you here alone. Pack some things. We'll head up the ridge first, find Luke and Anna and let them know what's going on."

Sarah relaxed some and let him go, she bit her lower lip but said nothing. Daniel went to the low chest that stood at the end of the bed. He removed the quilt that lay on top, and opened the lid. Inside lay a worn, but neatly folded blue uniform, leather belt, and some paper packages. He stared for a moment, studying the box's contents, and then shut the lid; he slid the chest aside and studied the floor underneath. He placed a fingertip under one corner of the flooring and pulled up. Under the board lay some items wrapped in linen; he removed the top cloth, opened one end and gazed at the hilt of an officer's sword; he rewrapped it and put it aside. The other bundles he lifted and lay on the bed.

He unwrapped the larger cloth and withdrew a short-barreled carbine, placing it carefully on top of the folds. From the other, he pulled a pistol; Daniel balanced the weapon in his open palm, and studied it. The sunlight streaming in the window glinted off the cold blue metal of the barrel and shiny brass on the grip. Across the top of the barrel where the bullet started its flight, small square letters were stamped in the metal:

ADDRESS COL. SAML COLT NEW-YORK U.S. AMERICA.

He thought, *You have any complaints, there's the maker.* Spencer remembered the smooth, satisfying kick when the Colt's trigger was pulled – and how deadly accurate the piece could be. *What if it works too well? Who do I talk to then?* He felt Sarah standing behind him.

Sarah glanced at the pistol in his hands and then to him. "If going is not safe for me, then what about you…?" There was no answer. She looked down at the floor, shaking her head.

"Alright. If you've made up your mind," she said quietly, "You'll need food. I'll see what I can come up with." She turned to go downstairs.

Minutes later, Spencer had the weapons loaded, tucking extra rounds into his haversack. He tucked his military discharge papers into the side pocket in the event he encountered a Yankee provost outpost; if he encountered Rebels on the other hand, no clear solution came to mind. He placed another handful of cartridges in the haversack. He walked quickly down the stairs and put his pack and rifle by the door. Sarah stood at the table wrapping some items in a flour sack. Daniel noticed she had changed to a cotton shirt, and a pair of old trousers. *Sometimes she surprises...*

He smiled. "That's different. Not sure your father would approve..."

"You didn't think I would go sidesaddle did you?" she asked, but didn't smile. She sat down and pulled on her riding boots. "I've put up some of the bread and ham. It's not much, but I expect we won't be gone that long." Sarah raised her eyebrows and looked at him for confirmation.

He looked back, but no words came. He watched as she silently pushed the bag into the top of his pack. *Say something...*

"Look, Sarah..."

She shook her head and looked up at him. She lifted her chin as she did when her mind was set. "Daniel, this is not decided yet; there is more to be said. We can talk about it on the way to find Lucius and Anna." Sarah turned, opened the front door and walked onto the porch.

The puddles in the barnyard reflected a slate-blue sky. The early morning haze lay wet and late along the lane. Wisps of fog drifted up through the treetops on the hillside below; beyond, the sun was rising dully through the broad cloud that lay dark over the valley to the east.

The couple walked quickly to the barn; Sarah backed Tobey from the stall and fixed his halter lead to the tie rail. Daniel did the same with the Southern major's horse; the mare snorted quietly as he examined the wound on her back. Daniel nodded: the big animal had done well as could be expected with a day's rest, and Sarah would be a light enough burden. He put salve on the welt and soft padding over it.

They finished saddling the animals and led them out to the yard. Daniel pulled the reins in to steady the big mare. "She's a big animal, Sarah, but seems to be a lady. The sore on her back looks better, and you'll be a lighter ride. Come on, I'll give you a leg up."

Sarah stroked the mare's flank and said quietly. "She's a beautiful animal. We'll be fine, young lady, won't we?" She mounted and turned the horse about the yard, feeling her out.

Daniel took Tobey's reins and mounted. The couple crossed the yard and followed the narrow lane that ran uphill past the stone house. Above the wheatfield beyond, the way passed up into the woods toward the ridge above.

At the top of the lane, Daniel pulled up Tobey and looked about: the dark green and brown of the pines ahead contrasted sharply with the etched gold of the wheat and the blur of gray mist that rose from the valley. He breathed deeply of the rich air; he felt better, glad to be moving, going somewhere.

From behind him, Sarah said softly, "So beautiful here. Remember when we rode up here every Sunday?"

He nodded and thought back. *Seems like an age ago...* Far off in the pines, an owl cooed a descending scale, but otherwise the woods were strangely quiet. Even here, nature seemed to have fled the carnage below. Tobey snorted and shivered his coat; Spencer patted the animal's neck and led the way up the hillside under the pines. There, the damp ground made for slow going, the horses' hooves sinking noiselessly into the thick, wet layer of pine needles that carpeted the old lane. Not far along, the path rose more steeply as it climbed toward the crest. Unlike the foliage below, the trees on the exposed rise were thinner and more stunted, and beyond, rock ledges lined the summit. Spencer turned off the lane, leading them under the cover of the treeline, carefully eyeing the slopes as they rode. Against the deathly quiet, the sound of the animals' hooves on the rocky ground here sounded uncommonly loud.

Through the trees just below the crest, they could see the lane to the farm's high pasture; Luke and Anna should be nearby. Here the lane joined the old road that ran from the west side of the mountain to the eastern slope and finally to the valley below. An ancient stone wall bordered the path; at one time a fairly substantial stack, the stones now lay tumbled down and vines spread freely over the rocks.

Spencer looked at the roadbed; plainly visible were hoof prints and the ruts made by iron-rimmed wheels. He wondered. *Could be Luke and Anna... Or Rebels.* To be safe, they kept to the woods that lined the road as they made their way downslope. The air underneath the trees was warm and humid. Here and there, tall patches of brambles grew up between the branches, and they had to lay flat behind the horses' necks as they made their way underneath the tangle.

Spencer froze. From the thick brush in front of them, came the metallic *shuck-shuck* of a repeating rife going to full cock. He pulled up Tobey, and sat stock-still. A voice boomed out from the tangle of brush that lined the edge of the lane.

"Now if that horse weren't so sorry-looking, I would have shot you already. But I felt bad for whatever poor soul might be riding such an animal... Hello there, Captain Spencer."

Daniel squinted into the thatch of green and yellow leaves ahead. Just ten feet away, Lucius Hand stood up from the brush, tall and barrel-chested, with a broad smile on his face; he raised the long barrel of the Henry rifle into the air and uncocked the weapon. Daniel blew a long breath between his lips, and relaxed.

"Damn, Luke. You likely aged me ten years. And I left the officer's rank behind a while ago."

Luke chuckled and walked from behind the brush, all the while gazing carefully around. "Didn't mean to give you cause, Daniel; can't be sure the Rebs are gone yet. And callin' you Captain? I'm afraid you still got that soldier's look about you, 'specially when you're prowling around like you were. Just as well you didn't surprise Anna. She's got that scattergun over there. I behave myself when she's toting that thing."

From behind another tree Anna had appeared: equally tall, with high, proud cheekbones, piercing hazel eyes – and hefting a shotgun. The couple smiled at each other, Anna picking up her chin and wincing at Lucius as if still considering her options. She then turned to the Spencers and studied the couple carefully.

"Morning to y'all. Anything wrong?" Anna looked at Sarah with concern. "You okay honey?"

Sarah managed a smile, and nodded. She dismounted and hugged Anna. Luke looked to Daniel, the same question on his face. Daniel dismounted, taking off his hat and pushing his matted hair back. "No, nothing's wrong. Things haven't been too bad, Luke. How are you two? You've been okay?

"Well, we had a shaky moment or two, but haven't seen Rebs this side of the ridge in a couple of days. There was a hell of a thing goin' on over to the Monterey Pass a couple nights ago, but it was rainin' so hard, I 'spect it came to nothin' for either side."

Luke walked over to the black mare and placed this hand on the *C.S.* brand on her flank. He turned to Daniel and cocked his head. "A Rebel mare? Well now. I imagine there's a story here. Hm?"

Spencer stared at the ground impatiently, thinking. *I need to go...*

He looked back at Luke. "It's all a long story, Sarah can fill you in. We came up here because I need a favor, Luke. Like you say, I think the Rebs have gone west of the mountain, so I'm headed down to Gettysburg to check on Rebecca. While I'm gone, I'd like Sarah to stay with you two."

Sarah had dismounted. She turned and stared at him, her chin raised stubbornly. "That's not going to work Daniel. I am going to go with you. She's my sister. I am going with you."

Luke and Anna looked at each other, then back at the Spencers. After a moment, Anna gazed at Daniel with her eyes narrowed as if she was looking at something far beyond him. She spoke guardedly. "Now, Daniel Spencer, no matter who's going or isn't, what in damnation you looking to go into that valley for? I caught the breeze from down there at sunup; ole man Death been busy down there…"

He nodded at Anna and smiled. "I'll be fine Anna. The Wagamans want me to see if Rebecca is okay. And I want to find out what happened."

Anna frowned at him. "Miss Becky? Sakes alive! If anyone knows how to take care of herself, she does. You best worry about any Rebs fool enough to give that girl trouble! And things down there be just fine without you. What? You missing that war? Mr. Daniel, you done your time, an' Lord knows you done more than most. Why don't you stay up here with the living and…"Anna stopped mid-thought. She sighed.

"No, your mind's made up isn't it? You do what you have to. But you, Sarah. I've been on a battlefield after they got done killin'. There's nothing you ever want to see there. Your man will have an easier time not worryin' about you. You stay with us. We'll help you get things back in shape on the farm."

Spencer turned to Sarah. "Please, Anna's right. I can move faster on my own. I shouldn't be gone much more than two or three days. In the meantime, you can do more good up here. Will you do this for me?"

Sarah bit her lip and looked away. "I don't like this at all. Not at all. With all that has happened, I'm worried about you," she looked back at him, still thinking. "But alright, I'll stay. Find my sister and come back as soon as you can." She turned and embraced him.

"But how do you feel? I'm still worried about…" She stopped.

He held her and whispered, "It will be okay, Sarah."

Spencer turned to Luke and spoke quietly, "As I said, it looks like Lee's army has already gone west. So any Rebs still around here are probably deserters and likely up to no good. When you get back to the farm, you have any problems with Rebs – *any problems* – you shoot first and discuss it later. They won't give you a second chance."

Luke nodded. "We'll take care of things, Daniel, don't you worry. Do what you have to and come back safe. Tell you what, we been ready to head back; just take us a few minutes to collect the animals. How 'bout you wait for us over to the top of the road where there's some cool air. You can head down the old valley road from there and we'll go with Sarah back to the farm."

Spencer wanted to get moving. *Now…*

Sarah came up behind him and whispered, "Yes, I know you're ready to go; but since I'm not going with you, a few minutes alone would be nice."

He thought a moment. Whatever happened in the valley, a few minutes more wouldn't make a difference. Daniel nodded to Sarah. The four agreed to meet at the top of the lane within the hour. The Hands headed downslope to their camp; Daniel and Sarah mounted and left the treeline, riding slowly in the close air, following the old road toward the crest.

They had ridden but a short distance up the path when Tobey began a low whinny. Spencer heard movement close behind him.

"Don't move, Yank," a low voice drawled. The barrel of a musket poked up hard at the old scar on Daniel's ribs. He grimaced at the prodding, and then raised his hands.

"We mean you no harm. We're civilians."

"Ah see. But then, ah don't really give a shit what you are, mister. Now. I want you both to get down slow. Anything funny, someone gets shot real quick."

Daniel looked at Sarah. "Do as he says." They dismounted slowly.

"Turn round slow, you Yankee son of a bitch," growled a second voice.

Spencer kept his arms in the air and turned. There stood two Rebels, their gray uniforms almost unrecognizable under the dirt, but the barrels of their rifles glinted at hip level; they uneasily eyed the couple, perspiration beading on their faces. The shorter one reached out, yanked Spencer's pistol from the holster, and held it up to study it.

"A civilian, eh mistah? This here's an Army Colt," he said, "Looks like mebbe you also done some fighting." The Southerner pushed the piece under his belt.

The other Rebel, a large man with expressionless eyes, walked up behind Sarah and whipped off her hat.

"Well, lookee here, Poot. Damned, if this Yank ain't a woman. Purty too…" The Rebel leaned in and smelled Sarah's hair, then hooked two begrimed fingers under the top button of her blouse and pulled it out as if to look inside.

Sarah pushed his hand away, and spun around. "Get your hands off me, you rebel pig!"

Daniel started, but the smaller Rebel cocked his musket.

"Ah said don't move, Yank… Now Ty, leave her be. We're jest here for them horses." The larger Rebel scowled at him, but turned away from Sarah and began to look over the mare.

Under the grime, the first Southerner was a smallish young man with narrow eyes and a wispy goatee. He looked at Sarah. "Look Missy, we aim to take your animals and such and go on our way. You want to be included in that list of what we take, you jest keep mouthin' off." He turned back and studied Daniel. "So, mister. Where you headed all the way up here?"

Spencer spoke quietly, but firmly. "We're civilians, Reb. We mean you no harm. It's very simple. We live near here. We're headed to check on family."

Behind them, the larger Rebel had put down his rifle and was leaning over, studying the mare's flank. "Hey Poot, this here's a Confederate brand." He narrowed his eyes at Daniel. "Wonder what happent to the man who owned him?"

The goateed man pointed the rifle closer to Daniel's chest and winced. "Well, well. Git your hands up higher, Mister. Once agin, mebbe things ain't so simple as you say. Tell me 'bout that horse and be quick about it."

"He's right, far as it goes," Spencer said, "The mare belonged to a major in your army named Stanton. He lost a leg in the battle and he came to our farm for help. He died yesterday. We buried him on our farm."

The Rebel looked uneasily from Daniel to Sarah. "Ah see. Mebbe so, mebbe not. Don't give a shit one way t'other – jest one less officer to worry about."

The Rebel turned, grinned at the other, and laughed. "Our army, Ty? Don't rightly know about it being *our* army anymore, do you? At the moment, we're detached you might say." They both chuckled.

"Deserters, you mean…" Sarah muttered.

The bigger Rebel walked back over to Sarah. "We told you to shet up!"

He grabbed her arm and pulled her towards him. Sarah screamed and raked at the man's face with the nails of her free hand. Infuriated, he grabbed the front of her blouse with both hands and threw her roughly to the ground, tearing open the shirt's front. The man stood over Sarah, leering at her breasts while he held his hand to his bleeding cheek.

"Goddamn Yankee bitch! Poot? Got some nice 'uns here. I'm thinkin' a piece of this tail might jest suit me after all." He started to unbutton his trousers.

All in an instant there was a roar; the horses reared and kicked, leaves fluttered down amidst the smoke that rose from the bushes beside the lane. The large Rebel lay dead on the ground, his chest a mass of blood and torn tissue. At the gunshot, the goateed man turned to see what had happened. It was enough. Spencer grabbed the barrel of the Rebel's rifle and lifted, jamming the butt end hard into the man's throat. The Rebel looked oddly surprised for a moment, but then fell back, gasping for breath. He lay on the ground, his hands moving up and down, undecided whether to grab the pistol at his waist, or clutch at his crushed windpipe for a breath. Spencer made the decision for him: he pulled the Colt from the Rebel's belt and stood back, aiming the piece at the Southerner.

"Kill him!" Sarah cried. She stood up, pulling her torn blouse to cover herself. "Kill him!" She started to pick up the other Rebel's rifle, tears of rage down her cheeks.

Anna Hand stepped into the lane from the brush, the still-smoking shotgun pointed at the dying Rebel. "Easy honey," she said, "I don't think these boys be hurtin' anyone real soon." The man at Anna's feet clutched at this throat, shivered once more, then lay motionless.

Daniel holstered the Colt and ran to Sarah, pushing the rifle she held into the air, and wrapped his arms around her. "Shhh. It's over, Sarah. They're dead. It's over. Are you hurt?" She shook her head as she leaned into his arms. Daniel held her close and rocked her as her sobs slowed.

Lucius had appeared from up the lane, Henry rifle at the ready, eyeing the trees on either side of the lane. "Jes' these two? They alone? Daniel, you two okay?

Spencer caught his breath. "Yes, looks like they were alone. And we're okay thanks to Anna and you. Thank you both..."

Luke uncocked the rifle and lowered it. "We saw fresh tracks down the road headed this way," he said, "Knew somethin' was up. Glad we came back."

Anna stood in the road, staring at the dead men at her feet. Her voice was shaking now. "So Cap'n, this what you meant about shootin' first and askin' questions after? 'Fraid these two don't have much to say..."

She uncocked the other barrel of the scattergun and let it fall to the ground. She wavered on her feet. Luke rushed over, and held her shaking in his arms. For some moments, the humid slope was still again: two couples embraced under the trees, two men lay dead in the road.

By mid-morning, the Rebel deserters lay in shallow graves on the ridge. Spencer led the way back to the farm, riding in first to check the house and the barn. Everything was as they left it; he gave two whistles, and from up the hill, Sarah and Anna emerged with the wagon; Lucius rode the mare behind, leading the animals – and holding the Henry rifle with the stock resting on his thigh.

Spencer tied Tobey to the porch rail and walked to the cistern on the end of the springhouse; he took a long drink from the dipper and cupped cool water over his neck and face. He recalled filling the major's canteen here; the two days that had passed seemed ages before. *You need to go, but...* He stood and watched concerned as Sarah climbed off the wagon.

Lost in thought, she had started up the front steps, but turned, caught his look and stopped. "I'm fine, Daniel. I'll be right back." Sarah went into the house.

Lucius began taking the animals to the barn and corral; Anna was already pulling boxes from the wagon and placing them on the porch. She stood, wiping the perspiration from her forehead she looked at Daniel, sensing his concern.

"We talked some, Daniel. She took a fright, but I think she's okay now. I'll keep an eye on her, don't you worry." Anna frowned at him.

"Now unless you want to help us put things away, you best get going."

Sarah reappeared onto the porch above them. She had changed into one of Daniel's shirts and now stood watching him, her eyes that deep blue. "Anna's right, you know. If you're planning to go by yourself," she said, "Go, before I change my mind." She walked down the steps and kissed him hard.

"Find my sister safe," she said, "If she needs anything, tell her she is always welcome here." Sarah kissed him again quickly, but held onto him.

"Daniel," she whispered, "I know you need to do this, so I won't say any more. Except, take care. I will be waiting for you. No, things haven't been right, but we can fix them." She looked at him with her chin raised. "My love goes with you..."

Those words... He held her. *I waited so long to hear them; now I leave...*

"And mine with you," he whispered, "Please don't worry. I'll be fine... Be back as soon as I can." Daniel turned, unhitched Tobey and swung up into the saddle. He nodded to the Hands. "Luke and Anna, thanks again. Take good care." He pulled the reins to the left and rode down the mountain.

PART II

Coming Home

July 6, 1863: Midday
Valley at Carroll's Tract, Pennsylvania

The paths of Lee's retreat west through the mountain passes were dead zones watched by both armies: men beyond exhaustion who had little problem shooting one more man, uniformed or otherwise, foolhardy enough to appear between the lines. Daniel assumed the main routes, through Cashtown to the north or Fairfield below, were a risky course. Instead, he decided to follow the mountain streams that fed the Spencer sawmill to the lowland that lay between the two roads; there, Little Marsh Creek as it had come to be known, ran east across the valley and eventually met the main flow of Marsh Creek just outside of Gettysburg. With some luck, he could work his way between the two armies; once behind the Union advance, he could head directly to Gettysburg to find Rebecca – and an answer to questions he couldn't quite frame.

Over the millennia, the run-off that formed the creek had carved a narrow defile through the east side of the mountain. Nearby, the old Jack Road paralleled the run all the way down to the Spencer Mill and the valley below. Staying out of sight, Spencer threaded a path down the rocky banks to where the creek ran white and fast with the recent rains. Through the trees, the mill buildings appeared to have been emptied, but were largely intact. Even so, he kept to the wooded banks, reining Tobey as close to the edge of the swift current as he dared. Business would have to wait for another day.

At the edge of the lowlands, a small stone bridge spanned the creek where the main road led south to Fairfield. Spencer studied the roadway and fields beyond. For the moment, the path appeared empty, but the ground had seen recent traffic: the once-packed dirt of the roadbed had been churned to mud; the neat fence posts that lined the road remained, but the rails they once cradled lay charred in the campfire rings that blackened the fields beyond. Beside the road, short pieces of plank stood in counterpoint to the uprights, marking dark mounds of freshly turned earth like so many crooked teeth.

He reined Tobey slowly by, gazing at the rough markings in the wood:

D. Root, 7 Vrg. CaV

Jos. Budray, 6 Virg. Cvry.

Rebels. Poor Rebel bastards. Come all the way here to die in the mud... It crossed his mind again now: who are these men, these enemies?

In all the carnage of the killing fields, Spencer had always somehow managed to keep death at arm's length – *or a gunshot's*. The Southern major and the two deserters on the mountain were different: one way or another, Spencer had been part of their deaths. They were poles apart as human beings, he decided, but like enough in one respect: trying to get home as best they could. Stanton at least died peaceably. *But regrettably...* Then he recalled the surprise on the deserter's face when he crushed his windpipe. *I damn well wanted him to die...* But an honorable warrior or a brutal opponent? Was the only difference their motivation? *Still...some mother's son...*

He pulled up Tobey, leaned on the pommel of the saddle and looked back at the mountain. *Honorable?* He shook his head. *Stop this shit... What difference is honor if all are dead? No one gets home...* He pulled at his collar and swallowed drily. He turned east again, picking up Tobey's gait to clear the open ground and return to the low banks of the run.

Further downstream, a farm lane crossed the creek and turned to parallel the water's course. At the ford, Spencer urged the horse up the bank and warily followed the path. Ahead the lane turned where it met the eastern edge of the valley; the Henshy family owned this farm, old friends whose large house and bank barn sat on the hillside. He turned off the road and slowly followed the cow path that led to the barn; he reined in Tobey at the edge of the building and peered into the farmyard.

The family had fled; the contents of their home lay strewn about the muddy ground as though shaken out of the doors and windows that stood open and silent. The only sign of movement came from a curtain that waved from one window and a gaunt horse that slowly hobbled to the water trough. The gelding had oozing saddle sores, and but three legs, the remaining limb hanging at an odd angle from the tangle of blood and tissue that remained at the joint. *Someone's used up cavalry horse...*

Daniel rode across the farmyard, the animal's glazed eyes following him in silent rebuke as he passed. *A gunshot will draw attention, don't risk it...* Daniel stopped and looked back at the horse. *The animal did nothing to deserve this pain...* He tied Tobey to the fence rail at the edge of the yard, and slowly walked back to the wounded beast. He spoke quietly to the horse as he rubbed its forehead, blocking the animal's view as he drew the Colt; he removed his hand and quickly fired a single shot.

By mid-afternoon, Spencer reached the maple-shaded ford of Marsh Creek without incident. He stopped at the broad shallows and dismounted under the trees. While Tobey drank deeply of the cool water, Spencer ate some of the ham Sarah had packed for him. He knelt at the bank to refill his canteen and looked about. He had last forded there years before, but the place had changed little: the creek gathered speed here, and poured through a jumble of moss-covered boulders; the air he drew in was thick with their wet, green smell. Just above, the wheel for Trostle's mill still turned, its creaking the only sound to be heard in the glen. Spencer remounted, and fording the swift stream, headed north past the silent buildings.

Now in the open, he took more caution. Just beyond Marsh Creek, he knew the road forked and he could follow the mill trail east toward Gettysburg. Rounding the last bend, Spencer pulled up abruptly: at the intersection stood a group of dismounted horsemen, one of whom raised his carbine. *Too late. Don't run...* Spencer stiffened, but then spied a Federal cavalry pennant and patches of blue showing through otherwise mud-covered uniforms. *Our boys.*

Nonetheless, two of the troopers eyed him carefully, holding their carbines at the ready. Behind them, the other men could not have cared less about a lone rider: two tended their mounts while yet another squatted tending a small fire under a coffeepot. Spencer reined Tobey slowly toward them.

"Ho, there mister. Jes' come ahead and keep 'er slow."

Spencer raised his hands in acknowledgment and rode slowly toward the speaker, a short grizzled man with faded sergeant's stripes.

"So what's yer story there bud?"

"Name's Spencer. I have a farm here, over toward the mountain. Heading to Gettysburg looking for family. Have my papers here if you like, Sergeant. I served with the 107th Pennsylvania up 'til this year."

He kept one hand in the air, and with the other slowly pulled the folded papers from his pocket and handed them to the sergeant. While the man thumbed the pages, Daniel studied the rest of the group. Grim, expressionless faces showing sunken eyes. *Used up... These men have been through hell.* Even covered in mud, Spencer could see their mounts were thin and just short of worn out.

The sergeant folded the papers and handed them back. "Thankee, Cap'n. Seen any Rebs?"

"Had a run-in this morning with two stragglers on the mountain. They're the worse for the experience. Otherwise, no. Far as I can tell, looks like the Rebels have gone west into the passes. Is Lee beaten? Did Hooker do it?"

"Hooker? Ha! Gin'ral Hooker's done and gone. Hard to keep track of 'em ain't it? 'Twas Gin'ral Meade won this. Yup, looks like Lee is retreating." The sergeant squinted toward the mountain, scratched at his whiskers and smiled, as if wishing the Rebels good riddance. He looked back at Daniel and shrugged.

"I 'spect so anyway, never know what Bobby Lee will do," he said. "Wail sir, you cain head on through – you best be careful though."

"Sergeant, as I say, I was with Reynolds' First Corps. Know where they are?"

By now, the other troopers had turned to look at him. The sergeant studied him more carefully.

"Wail sir, far as I know, the First Corps has gone south like most everyone else. Tell you were they was though: a few days back they had the devil's fight with the Rebs north of town. Gin'ral Reynolds himself was killed, and I hear those boys got shot all to hell and back; so you'll find their hospitals there still, just about two miles over that way. But things aren't quite settled along this here north road yet, Cap'n."

The sergeant hooked his thumb over his shoulder at the mill road leading east. "Might save you bein' shot accidental-like if you head that way first, then go north."

"That's where I'm headed," Spencer said, "Thanks Sergeant. Good luck." He nodded at the rest of the group, rode away, turning up the road toward Gettysburg. What had happened there still loomed as an unknown, but one thing was clear to him. *They got shot all to hell... I left them and they got shot all to hell.*

I should have been there...

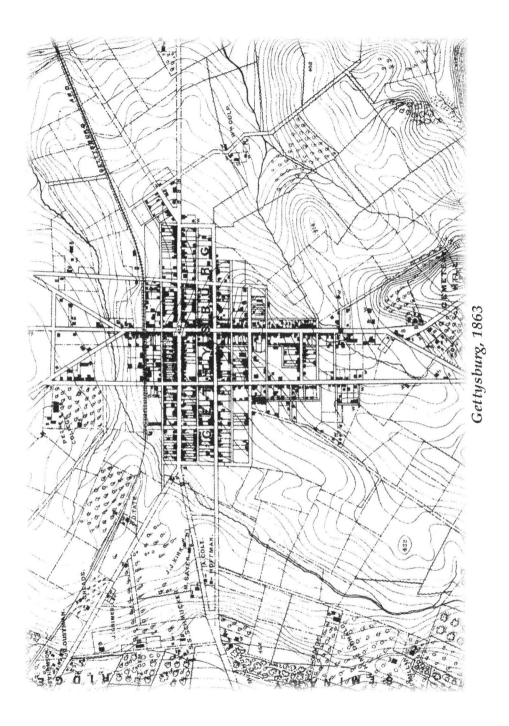

Gettysburg, 1863

July 6, 1863: Afternoon
Herr's Ridge, West of Gettysburg

The faint tang of burnt gunpowder had drifted in the valley air all morning, but as Spencer rode up the slope, the sulfurous smell mixed with the stench of the dead; the rank air blew toward him like a breath of some hell. Tobey snorted, turned his ears back. *We must be close.* He remembered Anna's words from that morning: *Death been busy down there...* He closed his eyes. *Indeed, it holds this ground with dark hands...* Daniel shook off the image, and patted the horse on the neck, whispering, "Come on old man, nothing here we haven't been through before."

Ahead the ground rose steadily toward a substantial ridge and a crossroad. Here Spencer dismounted, unfastened the canteen from his saddle, and rinsed the sour taste from his mouth as he looked about. The lane to the left led north up to the Herr place on the turnpike, and to the south, the road ran to Bream's Tavern on the road to Fairfield; but the quaint intersection he recalled of tight rail fences was almost unrecognizable. The passage of countless iron-rimmed wheels had left the roadbed knee-deep in churned mud and ruin: cut from their traces, dead horses and mules lay half-buried in the drying filth, flies swarming about their eyes and muzzles. Scattered all along the mired roadbed lay soiled blankets and rags crusted with dried blood. Here and there beside the lane, more untidy uprights of slat and board poked from freshly turned earth, already faded scratches and pencil marks the only clue as to who lay beneath.

He turned north, riding toward the brick house and stone barn of the Herr family; compared to the desolation behind, the area around the great bank barn was a beehive of activity. In the yard and around the sides of the building, windrows of Rebel wounded lay in varying degrees of misery. Here and there, shirt-sleeved orderlies slowly picked their way among them with buckets of water. On the back porch of the main house stood a young woman, the apron and the hem of her dress smeared with blood. She held her wrist to her forehead against the afternoon sun, gazing across the fields, as if looking for something – anything – that might remedy the despair that surrounded her.

Spencer skirted the farm and outbuildings and made his way cross-lots to the main road. Ahead a deserted tollhouse marked the far outskirts of Gettysburg; beyond, the turnpike crested a series of ridges that lay west of the town. He noted the apple and cherry trees bordering the road had an odd, twisted look. *Like hell has blown through...* Despite the chastened landscape, so far the fields here shared little of the devastation he remembered in Virginia. Then he crested the rise.

The cornfields that once stood on either side of the road lay flattened; a few stalks remained with leaves hanging limply, the lost survivors of some disaster. Dead horses and cattle dotted the field, rank and grotesquely bloated after days in the sun. And scattered as far as the eye could see, the detritus of war: pieces of uniform, torn cartridge papers, filthy blankets, broken weapons; in the dirt closer at hand, his eye fell on more personal items: a pair of broken eyeglasses, scattered pages of a letter, a muddied Bible.

The darker soil marking fresh graves scarred the ground for acres. Here and there, stooped men with spades hacked at the sodden earth yet; tired, unhurried motions repeated far too many times. Several dead still lay where they had fallen days before, now nameless mounds of dark swollen flesh. *Some mother's son...*

The afternoon sun burned through the low clouds, and the small breeze that had stirred the pall disappeared; foul, humid air closed in and pulled at the top of his stomach. A familiar sense of dread rose in Daniel's chest, but his dark memories were a pale comparison to this butchery. The horror here raked at his resolve. *My God... What kind of hell is this? What answers can you possibly find here...? Turn around. Get away...*

He needed to move. *Anywhere. Keep moving...* He spurred Tobey to a faster gait up the pike. Ahead was the Lutheran Seminary and the last ridge above Gettysburg; there he could get a view of town. Months before, Spencer had seen the ruin of Fredericksburg after the battle; he expected no less here. *But you need to know. You will...*

He rode over the crest and stopped, pinching his eyes with one hand, trying to focus: below, more whitewashed fence posts lined the road, stripped of their rails, and the fields had the same blown-down look of the Virginia landscape; but beyond, the buildings of Gettysburg still stood. *Not burned. I'll be damned...* He reined Tobey down the slope.

"Spencer! Dan Spencer!" In the yard of a gabled brick house north of the turnpike, a bandaged figure waved and limped toward the road.

"Spence', hell and damnation, is that you?"

Daniel pulled the reins up and looked at the man blankly; the face looked vaguely familiar.

"It's me, Jim Corcoran! The 107th! How in blazes are you here?"

Holy shit...Corcoran. Company C... Spencer thought back: the lieutenant had managed to get through Antietam in one piece; now he looked like he had been through hell. A stained bandage swathed his head, another wrapped his calf, and his right arm was in a sling; he was gaunt and long in need of a bath.

"Good God. Corcoran? Are you...alright?"

"Oh hell, looks worse than it is," Corcoran grimaced, "Least I can get around; plenty here have much worse. But Spence? Thought you were still in a hospital – some even said you died."

"Died?" Spencer dismounted, and shook the lieutenant's good hand. "No. Had pneumonia; it chewed at me awhile, but I got through it. Hell, I'm glad you're up and about, Jim. Tell me: I hear the Corps got hit hard. What about the 107th – how'd they make out? Is the regiment still here?"

Corcoran looked across the road, gazing into the field beyond for a few moments. "Well, can't say as I know much about that. I hear the Army has moved South; imagine the regiment went with 'em." He pointed with his thumb to the trees that lined the ridge beyond the house. "We *were* up there on the other side of those woods," he said distantly, "Fought like hell, but got flanked. Probably lost over half...lots captured. Anyways, I was wounded...was only with the regiment the first day. Can't say what happened after that."

He looked up at Spencer and smiled, "But goddammit, Spence, by the end we licked 'em. Lee retreated." Corcoran gazed toward the house. "There's a couple of my boys here. Doing the best I can for them. And I best tell you now: your man Quinn was wounded too. Bad. I've seen him; he's just up the road a bit." Corcoran nodded toward town. "Can take you there if you want."

Spencer pulled his hat off and combed his fingers back through his wet hair. *Lost over half... Quinn wounded. Bad...how bad?* He shook his head and said, "Don't you bother yourself. I'm looking for family here already, but if you'd tell me where he is, I'd like to see him."

"Well, alright." Corcoran shifted his weight about on his good leg and turned, wincing as he pointed up the road. "I tell you what: the whole damn town is pretty much a hospital, but there's only one Catholic church. Quinn is there. Spence? I best tell you now: the man was lying on the field for three days, then they had to take his arm off. Well. He was awake last night when I was there, but..."

Corcoran stopped and rubbed at the stubble of whiskers on his chin. He stared up the roadway, and nodded, "Don't worry, Spence, Quinn's one tough bastard. Give him my best."

Spencer stared off up the road as well; his eyes welled. "Thanks Jim. Look, you take it easy; go lie down will you? I'll check back on you and the boys later."

Corcoran waved and hobbled back across the yard.

Daniel gathered the reins and swung into the saddle. The feeling returned: *While I sat at my fireplace, Quinn lay out there wounded. I should have been here...* Unsettled by the moans coming from the house, Tobey shivered his mane; without prodding, the horse headed quickly up the graveled road. Daniel heard Corcoran's words again, "Some even said you died..."

Maybe I should have...

July 6, 1863: Late Afternoon
Gettysburg

At the edge of the town stood a cluster of older white clapboard homes and beyond, neat brick rowhouses. Several of the buildings there held wounded as well, and the street in front of each structure hummed with the same unease, reflecting the turmoil within. From one frame house, a soldier in shirtsleeves leaned out the front porch and cast a bucket of crimson liquid into the road; next door, a dour-faced old man leaned from a second story window and tossed bloody rags into the yard below. From another home, a pale young woman turned up the street carrying an armful of linen and a carpenter's tray full of medicine vials. A slight breeze blew up the street, thick humid air that smelled of wet wood, churned earth, manure – and over all, something more organic and foul.

Daniel turned off the rutted main street, heading for the church he knew to be a block or two away to the south. He remembered St. Francis' location well enough: Becky taught at the Public School just up High Street. First, he wanted to find Quinn – and perhaps some more answers. *But what question do I ask...* Turning up the street toward the church, he could see the road ahead was in chaos: white-canvassed supply wagons squeezed between surreys and flat-bedded drays loaded with wounded men, their uniforms indistinguishable for the blood and filth; nuns with white-winged cornettes crossed the road in a flock, dodging sweat-soaked men with wheelbarrows and armloads of crates.

Just outside the crowd, he noticed toward a smallish tow-headed boy, blankly watching the confusion from the front step of a frame house across from the church. Daniel rode over.

"Hey there, what's your name?"

The boy scratched indifferently at the muddy ground with a stick. "Elliot," he said without looking up.

"You live here, Elliot?"

The boy looked up at Spencer, squinting into the glare, but his eyes showed little interest and less emotion. He gestured up the road, but said nothing.

"Well, I need to see a wounded soldier in that church over there. This is my horse Tobey. Will you watch him while I'm inside?"

The youth pursed his lips, stirring a circle in the mud with the stick. He spoke coolly, and almost to himself, "A wounded soldier. I know all about wounded soldiers. My pa is gettin' five dollars each to bring them up to the train station in our wagon…" He squinted up at Daniel, hoping perhaps for a comparable sum to watch a horse.

Spencer stared hard at the boy. *Quinn lay wounded in the rain…* He watched the youth shrug and frown at losing his imagined windfall. He dismounted and tied Tobey to a ring post; he thought for a moment. *The father charges wounded men money… And the boy is bartering to watch an animal. What has happened to these people?* He stood above the boy with his hand on the Colt; he glowered at the youth.

"Tell you what, boy. I was a captain with this Army. Just maybe I can have your father arrested. Or worse. No, I don't have any five dollars for you. I'll give you two bits to watch my horse and gear for a few minutes. No more. Think you can do that or not?"

The boy looked up with his eyes opened wide, suddenly aware he had angered the tall stranger who now stood over him; he stood up quickly and nodded agreement.

"Uh, yessir!"

"You know who's in charge here, boy?"

The youth quickly pointed to an officer, a gray-bearded man in a fresh blue uniform. "Uh, yessir. Yes I do. That man there been giving lots of orders. He just came in yesterday. Yessir, you do what you gotta do, Captain. I'll take good care of your horse awhile."

"Well. Thank you, Elliot. I'll pay you when I get back," he said, and turned on his heel. He smiled to himself. *Bullying children. Shame on you...* He made his way through the confusion; the officer was an older man, a major by his uniform, and stood thumbing through a sheaf of papers.

"Afternoon Major, may I have a word? Name is Spencer, formerly captain, 107th Pennsylvania. I'm trying to find one of my men."

The officer looked briefly at him and then back at the papers, shaking his head. "Well," he said, "You and everyone else, son." He waved the paperwork up and down. "Look at this mess; like trying to keep order in Purgatory. I can tell you this hospital here is mostly First Corps. You might want to ask one of the nurses here, they likely have a better idea of who is inside. Good luck."

Daniel thanked the officer and walked up the broad steps of the church. Just inside the double front doors, an operating table stood in the lobby lit by the afternoon sunlight. Those entering and leaving had to walk around the table where two doctors hunched over their unconscious patient, exploring the man's torn chest with long probes. At the back wall of the nave, a washstand had been placed, and a young nurse rinsed her hands there in the shallow basin. As Daniel walked over, she toweled them, staring at the blank wall in front of her.

"Excuse me miss, I was hoping you could help me. I'm looking for a man who may be here, a sergeant named Conall Quinn."

She looked up at him; he guessed her to be about twenty, pretty enough, but her wide-set brown eyes spoke of sorrow and exhaustion. She spoke hastily.

"Well sir, maybe I can help you, but I'm going to need your help first. I live up the street and you can help me with some food that needs carried. You can explain what you want on the way."

However, as they walked out of the church, it was she that talked though, nonstop and unselfconsciously, as the overtired will. She introduced herself as Sallie Myers, not a nurse as he had supposed, but a schoolteacher; yet she had been caring for the wounded of one army or another for most of the week. The Myers home was a few doors down, and also held a number of injured men that they had taken in; she led Daniel to the rear door so as not to disturb those who lay in the front parlor. As exhausted as she appeared, she walked quickly and moved with purpose, gathering bowls, spoons, and the food that her mother was preparing for the wounded. She pointed Daniel toward a large pot of hot soup, and a basket of fresh baked bread. She gathered the other items in a second basket and was already at the door.

"Watch it, that's hot. Alright. Let's go."

While they walked quickly back to the church, Daniel managed to introduce himself and asked again about Quinn. She thought for a moment, then she looked sideways at him.

"Let me think," she said. "Several soldiers named Quinn been through here, maybe yours. We will see in a minute. But Spencer...Daniel Spencer. Your name does ring a bell. Have we met?"

"No, I live out toward Cashtown. My sister-in-law lives here though, Rebecca Wagaman. I'm trying to find..."

"That's it! 'Becca? Goodness, I work with her here at the school; she's mentioned your family several times. Surprised you didn't see her. She's been helping at the church too."

I'll be damned... As they approached St. Francis, Daniel could feel the late afternoon sun hot on his back, but the activity around the church showed no sign of slowing down. From the far side of the street, the boy Elliot hallooed and waved as they passed.

"Hi, Mizz Myers. Hey, Captain, I'm still right here. Please don't arrest anyone."

Sallie waved at the boy and then turned to Spencer with a puzzled look. "We live neighbors to them. The child is a brat and his father is worthless, but whom are you arresting?"

"No one, no one," Spencer smiled, "It's a long story. He's watching my horse for me."

They climbed the church steps again and entered the lobby; Daniel noticed the soldier the doctors were operating on now lay covered with a stained sheet. Sallie looked quickly, but then turned her eyes to the floor.

"They just brought that boy in this morning from the battlefield. I was hoping they could help him..." She sighed heavily and walked to a narrow sideboard next to the doors, shaking her head.

"Please put the soup and such up on that table awhile. I'll give you some bowls... "

"Miss Myers, I'd be glad to help, but my friend may not have much time left either."

She looked at Daniel, closed her eyes and nodded her head. "That's right. I'm sorry, I'm just very tired. Quinn, right?" She called over a steward and spoke to him quietly; the man nodded and looked at Spencer.

"Maybe. Look up front by the altar. There's a sergeant up there they operated on yesterday."

"Thanks. Thank you, Miss Myers. I'll be back."

Beyond the foyer lay another level of hell. Even for one accustomed to the horrors of a field hospital, the interior of the church was an assault on the senses. Planks and doors had been placed across the pew backs; on them, hundreds of injured lay side by side, each man's agony in plain view and almost at face level. Sunlight slanting through three tall windows lit the humid air that rose from sodden cloth and anguished breath. Over the busy sound of traffic, neighing horses, and shouts that carried in from the street, a chorus of suffering rose almost as one voice. *That night at Fredericksburg...* But here inside, the walls of the church reflected some sounds: one moan might be heard briefly above the din, vying for attention, before falling back to the anonymous clamor.

He threaded his way through the nurses and attendants up the center aisle toward the altar. The vague sense of dread that had plagued him was gone; the capacity for the human body to withstand horrific injury and survive was all too clear. Daniel stopped beside the altar rail; he knew that Quinn had been badly wounded, but he was unprepared for what he found. The sergeant lay off to one side, a bandage of what appeared to be yellow gingham wrapping the stump of his arm above the elbow. Semiconscious, he shifted about uneasily on the makeshift mattress of blanket-covered straw. The face Daniel remembered for its composure and calm amusement was a mask of pain – and the man groaned piteously. *Oh God, do something.* An attendant came out of a room just off the chancel.

"Excuse me, Corporal, I need to talk to a doctor about this man."

The attendant looked at him with heavy-lidded eyes and then down at Quinn. "You'll have to wait," he said indifferently, "Afraid he's not the only man who needs help here, bud. Who the hell are you?"

Spencer felt the anger rise in his chest; he set his jaw, but stayed calm. He moved closer to the attendant and leaned in. "Well, *Bud*, who the hell do I have to be? If you need to know, name is Spencer, Captain, 107th Pennsylvania; this man served under me..."

The corporal gazed down at Quinn and sighed. He avoided Spencer's scowl.

"Sorry Captain. Look. We've only got two doctors here. I'm just an orderly and I haven't slept in two days. At least your friend has had surgery. I'll try to get you somebody. S'all I can do mister." With that, he headed back down the aisle. Spencer stared after the man.

"He's just tryin' to get through the day, Cap'n," Quinn rasped. His eyes were open but unfocused.

"Quinn! You're awake!" Spencer knelt beside the sergeant. "How are you doing, Conall? Can I get you anything?"

"Awake? How can I sleep with all this racket? But Cap'n? Thought I was dreaming. Didn't know what happent to you after Fredericksburg; heard rumors... Glad to see you." Quinn raised his eyebrows and rasped, "Other'n that, I could do with a measure of old Bushmill's." He cackled weakly, and then grimaced. "If the single malt is not in the offing, would be obliged for some water..."

"You found your sergeant, I see." Sallie reappeared at Daniel's side carrying a mug full of water. She knelt beside Quinn and lifted his head carefully.

"Here sergeant," she said softly, in almost a whisper, "This is fresh from the well and still cool."

Quinn drank eagerly, leaned back with a faint smile. "Was truly hopin' for that single malt, but this'll do just fine. Thankee, dear." The sergeant lifted his head again, and tried to focus his eyes on Sallie. "My, aren't you a breath of fresh air?"

She smiled. "Thank you, Sergeant. Now lay back down," she said gently and placed the mug by his good arm. "The water is here if you want more." Quinn lay back and closed his eyes. Sallie put the back of her hand to his forehead and looked at Daniel with unease. She stood up, and gestured for him to join her. He noticed she was wringing her hands unconsciously in her apron. She spoke quietly.

"I've about given up trying to predict what will happen by a man's appearance, but he's flushed and has a fever. I think there's infection. I don't know. I'll do what I can to help. I'll be back."

Daniel watched as she turned and headed quickly down the aisle. *What can she possibly do in all this?* He knelt by Quinn's side and looked over the crumpled figure; what remained of his shirt was filthy and stiff with dried blood, and the full, ruddy face he remembered was drawn and drained of color. Daniel's throat tightened; he gazed off toward the altar and tried to swallow. When he looked back Quinn's eyes were open and squinted blurrily at Daniel.

"A minute ago I was just getting' impressed with the help 'round here; now here *you* are." He cackled again. "No offense there, Cap'n."

He met Quinn's gaze, smiled and shook his head, "None taken." He offered the mug of water for him to drink again.

"Well. If I be stuck with this, so be it," Quinn rasped and managed a wink. He leaned forward and sipped eagerly from the mug, then lay back again with a groan. He soon fell unconscious, his eyes half-shut, and his mouth framing words without sound.

Daniel felt someone approach behind him.

"Hello, stranger."

He turned toward the voice. Another day, the young woman who stood before him might have passed for a younger Sarah; that afternoon, Rebecca looked like some much older relation. Dark circles lay under her large blue eyes, and her face was long with sorrow. Blood had splattered the front of her apron and two red drops showed on her cheek.

Daniel stood, taken aback at her appearance; then they held each other. As they did, he could feel her relax and sink into his arms. "Good God, Rebecca, let's sit you down somewhere." Daniel put his arm around her back and led her to a small bench by the side of the altar. "Sit here and rest for a moment before you fall down."

She collapsed against him. She said quietly, "Thought someone might be checking up on me – but when Sallie told me you were here, I couldn't believe it. I'm so glad to see you…" She clasped held his hands in hers, her face on his chest. She sat up slowly and smoothed back the hair that had fallen to her face. "I'm about done in; but, good Lord, there's still so much to do. All these poor men…" She stared wearily across the room, tears streaking her cheeks. She lifted her head, "I'm sorry. Just need a moment…"

Daniel unrolled his sleeve, wiping the tears and dried blood from her cheek. "Becky, if you could see yourself; you need more than a moment. You're no help to anyone if you collapse. Just sit for a minute. First, are you alright?"

She looked at him with a faint smile and nodded. "Yes, all considered, I'm fine. But I've been so worried about you all; my God, we've been hearing nothing but horrible stories about the Rebels ransacking the farms. Are my parents alright? Sarah?"

"Everyone is fine. Some close calls, but by the looks of it, we're better off than folks around here." Daniel spent a few minutes describing the less worrisome events of the week for her. As he did, Rebecca appeared to relax some; she closed her eyes, shutting out the horror around them, and leaned back against him again. He told her enough to calm her, then turned to her, "It's a big relief that you're safe, Becky."

She turned toward him, and said quietly, "I'm so glad you came. It's been a while; it's wonderful to see you." She focused on his face, her brow wrinkled. "But you look exhausted," she said, "And what aren't you telling me?"

Spencer feigned surprise and shrugged.

Becky sat up, shaking her head. "Well, you haven't said as much, but I heard that Sarah and you lost a baby; I'm so sad for you. And yes, there's the Dan Spencer I remember: keep it bottled up; and I'll only find out when it's turning you inside out." She sighed and gazed past him.

Barely visible above the tier of wounded on the pews, Sallie Myers moved rapidly up the aisle toward the altar. On seeing Daniel sitting with Becky, she raised her eyebrows and almost smiled. "I see you've found each other. At least something good has happened here."

Sallie knelt over the unconscious sergeant and felt his forehead again. She turned to Daniel and said quietly, "Well, Captain, I think I can do something for your Sergeant. We've brought a few men to my family's home to make them more comfortable; I'm sure we can make space for him." She looked down at Quinn, still wringing her hands. "Hopefully it will help."

The orderly Daniel had spoken to earlier reappeared at the altar with a wooden stretcher. Sallie turned toward the man, her soft demeanor changing entirely. "Thank you for fetching that, Corporal," she said firmly, "We can take it from here." The man shrugged and went back to his rounds.

Sallie looked at Rebecca, and then at Daniel; despite her exhaustion, she was determined. "Your friend is not a small man, but I think between the three of us we should be able to carry him."

As the two women prepared Quinn for the move, Daniel gazed unconsciously at the stretcher that lay beside the sergeant. The grain of the wooden handles was black with dirt and sweat; the frayed canvas between the rungs showed sign of previous patients: yet damp stains tinted pale pink to crimson. Without waking the sergeant, they carefully lifted the blanket he lay on from the straw onto the stretcher. With the two women at one end, and Daniel at the other, they carefully made their way from the horror inside the church through the chaos outside. The air outside was cooler now – still foul – but an improvement over that inside.

They walked slowly down the somewhat quieter street to the Myers house. The boy Elliot still sat across the road, watching them pass; Daniel whistled and called for him to wait outside with Tobey. The Myers home was a smallish two-story affair, but the interior indicated a family of some means: the front hallway held fine dark furniture and a matching railing bordered the broad staircase beyond. To the left stood a parlor, where five wounded men lay on blankets on the polished wood floor. Sallie led them up the hall to another room beyond, smaller but more formal than the first. Spencer supposed it was previously a dining room, but the table had been removed to accommodate the two injured soldiers that lay to one side of the doorway; a third pallet lay empty under the far window.

At the room's threshold, the hall narrowed and with difficulty, they made the turn. Sweat dripped from Daniel's forehead, and he could see that Rebecca and Sallie, already worn down from their exertions that day, were almost at an end. They lifted the corners of the blanket, and carefully hefted Quinn onto the pallet under the window. The sergeant groaned at this last movement, but quickly slipped back into unconsciousness. Stepping quietly around the other wounded, the three returned to the hallway. Exhausted, Rebecca and Sallie sat down side by side on the staircase, wiping perspiration from their faces, Sallie with her handkerchief, Rebecca with a sleeve.

"Lord," said Becky, "Guess...more tired than I thought." Catching her breath, she sighed heavily and started pushing her hair back from her temples.

"Oh, yes," Sallie said, "but your hair must be just right." She feigned a superior look.

"Of course," Becky laughed, "And you my dear, you look fetching yourself." Beyond exhaustion from hours of grim labor, the two women leaned on each other and laughed like schoolgirls. Each shushed the other to be quiet, but both continued, muffling the noise with their sleeves. Until the tears came.

Drained himself, Spencer leaned against the banister, watching the pair sob. "You two will need to get some rest, or we'll need a nurse for you as well." He excused himself and stepped outside. Seeing Spencer, Elliot walked over, leading Tobey behind him. "See Mister? I'm still here, but…" he looked around uncomfortably, "Well, it's getting late and I need to get home or I'll get a birching."

Spencer turned to the west; the sun was setting over Seminary Ridge. "Sorry, Elliot. I did take a long time, and you kept your word. Don't want you to get in trouble."

"I promised you two bits?" Spencer reached into his pocket and tossed him a silver dollar. "Will eight make us even?"

"You bet, mister!" The boy turned the bright coin over and over in his palm, his mouth open. "Thanks!" With that, the youth ran up the street.

Daniel watched the boy disappear into one of the frame houses; he rubbed Tobey's flank and tied him to the rail outside the Myers home. "Be right back old man." He stepped back into the hallway to find the Becky still sitting on the stairs, her head leaning on the banister, and her hands holding the balusters for support. He could hear Sallie Myers rapid chatter somewhere in the rooms beyond.

Becky looked up, her face flushed and her eyes still wet; she sighed and managed a small smile. "So, Mister – excuse me – *Captain* Spencer, you've found Becky Wagaman, and she's safe as she's going to be. What will you do now?"

What will you do now...? Daniel suddenly realized that he had little idea where to start. In the middle of a maelstrom, he had not only found Becky, but also Quinn and Jim Corcoran. Now he needed answers. Corcoran might have them.

"Well. Now that the sergeant is in good hands, I am going to ride back to the edge of town. I ran into another friend in a hospital over there. I want check on him again before it gets too late."

As Daniel spoke, Sallie returned from the back of the house. Her hands were still kneading unconsciously at her apron. "I didn't mean to eavesdrop, Captain Spencer, but if it will help, you can bring your other friend here. I will make room. We're about full up, but I will make room. Either way, before you go, I'll get you some food to take."

Daniel nodded. "I'm obliged Miss Myers. I'll see how he is feeling," As Sallie turned to go, he took her clenched hands between his. "You have been more than generous. I can't thank you enough for what you've done here." Sallie smiled shyly and then headed back to the kitchen.

Daniel turned to Rebecca. "Becky, I don't plan to be long. Where will you be?"

She thought for a moment. "I'll be at the church for a little longer. I'm exhausted but I'll wait for you here if you're coming back." She stood and hugged him. "And thank you for coming to town to see if I was alright. Be safe."

Sallie returned from the kitchen with a loaf of bread and small jar of apple butter. She pulled a piece of foolscap from the hall closet and wrapped the items. "You can bring this to your friend. If you're ready, 'Becca, we best get going too."

Daniel thanked her again and stepped outside. He put the paper wrap in his saddlebag, untied Tobey, and rode to the edge of town.

The sun was lowering behind the Seminary by the time Spencer reached the farm where he left Corcoran. A cool breeze blew from the north, thinning the heavy air. The lieutenant was still in the front yard, but was sitting back against a stack of supply boxes with his good leg drawn up; he sat motionless, his arms folded across the one knee, cradling his head. Daniel turned Tobey into the yard.

"Jim? You okay?"

The lieutenant sat up, his look confused and his eyes unfocused. It took a few moments for Corcoran to collect himself. "Spence... Hey, it's you," he rasped, "I was wondering if you'd get back. Just getting some shuteye out here where it's cooler." He grimaced as he started to stretch out.

"Don't get up, "Daniel said, "Let's sit a spell. I could use a minute too." He tied Tobey in the orchard beside the house to graze; he unhooked his canteen and pulled the wrap containing the loaf from his saddlebag. He handed Corcoran the canteen while he stood cutting the bread atop the boxes. The loaf was still warm.

Corcoran took a long pull from the canteen and then looked up with some curiosity. "Oh good Lord, is that apple butter?"

Daniel nodded, handing him a large slice; the lieutenant looked at it just briefly and smiled broadly before he devoured it. Spencer cut a small piece for himself and dipped it in the sweet butter. *Delicious.*

"How are you feeling?"

"Oh, I'm fine, I'm fine," Corcoran said, "So I'm doing what I can to help. The Sheads folks that own this place have been very kind. And we finally got these supplies, but these boys need alot more. Anyways, I'm doing what I can. Did you find Quinn?"

Daniel upended one of the wooden boxes, and sat down, filling Corcoran in on Quinn's condition and Sallie Myers' offer to help. He turned to the wounded man. "Jim, I think you should take her offer; maybe you could get better care there."

Corcoran pursed his lips, looked toward the Sheads' home; in the twilight, the candles glowed inside the open door and windows, and several groans echoed within. He slowly shook his head. "Thanks, Spence; and thank Miss Myers for me. As I said, I'm getting along fine. The Sheads family is very kind too. And I can be more help here."

"Had a feeling that's what you'd say," Daniel said, "Figured I'd offer. You said some of the 107th boys were here? Like to check in on them."

Corcoran nodded and led the way into the house, where they passed slices of the Myers' bread to any who could eat. Despite the open windows, the air was stifling and close. Spencer remembered clearly: the night hours were the worst; laying semi-conscious, the moans and tortured breathing of others become your own. One's thoughts wander between two horrors: an anguished present, and a doubtful future. He felt a wave of dread rise. *Move. Anywhere...* He started back outside suddenly, sat on the front step and held onto the railing. *Why did I survive?*

Corcoran hobbled along behind, somewhat puzzled. "You alright?"

"Sorry, yeah. Just tired. Kind of just hit me I guess." Spencer stood and stretched letting his eyes adjust to the dim. It was late. "Probably time I see how Quinn is getting along anyway." *Ask him...*

He turned back at Corcoran. "Before I go, I have a question for you," he said, "Maybe you'd just as soon forget, but can you tell me some of what happened? You and the regiment that first day? I'd like to know what happened to the boys."

Corcoran squinted at him in the half-light. "Well, can tell you what I remember, anyway." Dark was coming on, but Corcoran took his time, describing the regiment's long march north and arrival on the ridge north of the Seminary; but once the battle began, his memories became more jumbled.

"You know, I thought about this a lot while I've been here," he said, "Trying to put it in some kind of order, but the afternoon just doesn't add up. The Rebs hit us up there in front and then flank – or maybe it was flank first; not sure Spence, you know what I mean: time doesn't pass the same in a fight." He and sat on the step leaned back, thinking.

"Tell you one thing I won't forget: your man Quinn. He was hit early on by a piece of shell. MacThompson sends him to the rear to get patched. By then, I was wounded, and headed to the rear myself. But here comes Quinn, walking back up the ridge. Kept saying, 'One more shot, by God, one more shot…' Can still hear him sayin' that. Well, I told him to go to the rear again, but he says, 'Hell, L'tenit, there is no rear!' He was right, the damn Rebs had gotten behind us. Anyways, that was that – and the last I saw of Quinn until yesterday."

He closed his eyes. "Hell, you're lucky you got out when you did, Spence. Colonel Mac got shot, Captain Gish – we lost so many, I'm not even sure who was in charge at the end. Anyways, I passed out; next I know, the rest of the Corps was pushed back to the hills below town, and the Rebs captured me. Good thing they needed help with the wounded, otherwise I'd be headed south as a prisoner."

Daniel leaned forward; there was something missing. "Wasn't there something else? Wasn't there something that could have been done?"

"Something else?" Corcoran looked at him, puzzled. "Well, like I said, things are a little foggy. No matter how many we shot down, they kept coming. Our boys stood there and got shot down too. Seemed like the sun would never go down. No, nothing else we could have done." He smiled, "Anyways, Meade finally whipped 'em in the end."

Daniel nodded, but stared at the ground; there was still something missing.

Me...

"Sounds like you had the hell of a fight," Daniel said, "At least you did what you could... Sorry – sorry I wasn't there." He needed to be moving again; he stood up and stretched. "I best get going; and you need to get some rest. Thanks for your take on things."

Corcoran turned to him. "Now wait a minute. Spence'. Sorry you weren't there? I meant what I said: I'm glad you got out when you did. We caught hell that day, yes; but there's nothing you could have done to change that..."

Daniel stopped, staring into the darkness. "Maybe so. Won't know now, will we?" He untethered Tobey and mounted. "Take care, Jim," he said quietly, "I'll try and get back tomorrow."

March 15, 1863
Frederick, Maryland

His pace up the turnpike was unhurried. As much as he thought about getting home, it would take time to adjust – in attitude as much as location – from a war-ravaged landscape to a more tranquil setting. He found that getting there would take some doing: the land of central Maryland had little to spare over the ruin of Virginia.

The previous year, both armies had scoured the Maryland countryside for supplies. In the time since Antietam, Federal camps and hospitals had replaced many of the acres of farmland that once checkered the area; now several of the camps were abandoned, the ground filthy from overuse. He rode on past the wasted fields in silence. *Have we ruined everything?*

One way or another, what had become known as the "Mud March" that past January finished Spencer's military career. After his fruitless trek in the cold rain, the lingering cough from the night at Fredericksburg turned to pneumonia. The official resignation he had intended to submit was only a formality. By February, he was transferred to a hospital in Washington, so ill that the doctors there had signed his discharge from the army.

Spencer survived, but barely. Initially, he cared little one way or the other: one grew accustomed to waking to a day that only included the present; the future was a luxury for those not downwind of the killing fields. But as his health improved, he began to recall something of life without senseless bloodshed. *Home...*

Much to the surgeons' surprise, by the end of the month Spencer had recovered enough to walk the hospital grounds; as his strength grew, on warmer days he explored the streets of Washington. The enormous unfinished dome of the new capitol building loomed over an equally incomplete landscape of a city at war. Acres of tent-lined camps to train recruits, hastily built hospitals for those not strong, or lucky, enough to complete their service; enormous warehouses for the provisions necessary to wage the war, and sprawling depots for their transport to the front. Even as a veteran, Spencer marveled at the variety and quantity of supplies the Union had at its disposal. *Yet with all this, such a shortage of good judgment...*

With his health seemingly on the mend and discharge approved, Spencer made plans to leave for home. Still concerned about a relapse, the doctors recommended traveling by rail to avoid exposure. Spencer balked: trains were crowded, noisy and uncomfortable; the route north was a long, tedious ride up to Baltimore, then to the Susquehanna, and eventually west across Pennsylvania.

As it turned out, during one of his final walks around the capitol, Spencer happened on an injured gelding; one of the hundreds of dispirited animals destined for the slaughterhouse, the animal stood watching him from a corral fence. On closer inspection, he found the horse's injury had left it scarred and partially blind, but otherwise healthy. For a small bribe to a quartermaster sergeant, Spencer acquired the animal. The late winter weather had been mild; Spencer could make the trip home on horseback.

Then, with the journey only days away, the weather turned foul; the temperatures dropped and freezing rain coated the hospital windows. With reluctance, Spencer loaded his packs – and the horse he had named Tobey – onto the train to Baltimore. As expected, the ride north was crowded and slow; when the train did move, a chill draft blew through the cars. Supply trains further snarled the tracks north of Baltimore City, and the train halted for the night. It sealed Spencer's decision: he slept for a few hours in the baggage car, and at first light transferred to the rail line that led west to Frederick; from there he would make his own way home.

A mile from the Frederick spur, the wheel bearings of the tender began to smolder, and that train came to a grinding halt as well. Spencer had had enough. *Bullshit. What more can they do to me...* He ignored the conductor's protests and walked back to the freight car that held his belongings; there, the baggage-man protested as well, until Spencer put his hand on his Army Colt. For a brief moment, he gave second thought to his actions. *Why not? Just another son of a bitch keeping me from getting home...*

The conductor came up alongside, looking shocked. "You're a Federal officer, you won't shoot him..."

Spencer shrugged. "Now, did I say I'd shoot *him*?" He smiled at the conductor, and kept his hand on the pistol, tapping his finger on the wooden grip. Now thoroughly frightened, the conductor ordered the handler to open the car; he stood sheepishly while the man helped Spencer get the horse down to the siding.

Spencer smiled at the conductor. "Obliged for your trouble, gentleman," he said, "Such an efficient way to travel." He threw a gold dollar to the handler and headed north up the spur on horseback.

The chill rain had let up by the time he reached the outskirts of Frederick. Overlooking the city stood an old tollhouse, now occupied by a detachment of the Provost Guard; a lieutenant in an overlarge coat walked into the road. He studied Spencer, then saluted.

"Afternoon, Captain. Your orders, please?"

Spencer reined in, returned the salute, and handed down the documents.

The lieutenant looked briefly at the paperwork and handed it back to Spencer, looking wistfully at the folded pages. "A discharge. Headed home..." The man shook his head, "Haven't seen my family in a year."

Spencer tucked the fold back under his coat. "I could use a meal and some sleep. Any recommendations?"

"Well, Captain," he said, "Have to tell you, just had some folks pass through headin' out. They said any decent hotel not bein' used as a hospital was full up. Said they wouldn't put their mule up in the rest of the places. Lotsa' boys on leave, I guess: Army drovers with cattle and such. You can check, but I'd head further up the valley, sir." He saluted and waved for his men to open the tollgate.

Spencer rode down the broad slope toward the town. As the provost officer had described, Frederick was a madhouse. Near the center of town, the Pike crossed the old National Road, the broad path leading to western Maryland and to the frontier beyond. This day, the intersection was a snarl of carriages, wagons, cattle, and milling pedestrians. Along the main street beyond there were several hotels; all appeared overcrowded and noisy. Spencer was worn out, but it was early afternoon yet, and he was just as glad to ride on.

A few miles north of the city, he came to another crossroads at a small village. Units of both armies had doubtless passed through here; but the rural areas here in Maryland were a hodge-podge of sympathies, and by appearances, the inhabitants of this hamlet had raised the ire of one army or the other. The effect was the same: most of the buildings lay in piles of ashes and charred timber.

On the far side of the intersection, two buildings still stood: an ancient stone tavern and beside it, a ramshackle wood frame house with a wide porch. Spencer noted that the house leaned at such an angle that without the tavern's support, the whole affair would have collapsed like so many jackstraws.   While Tobey drank from the water trough beside the road, Spencer leaned on the tie rail and took his bearings. The turnpike north paralleled the high Catoctins; to the west, a few amber shafts of Jacob's Ladder poked through the clouds and dappled the mountainside below. Unlike the hard-surfaced National Road, his route home was less impressive: old planks lined the road in some stretches, packed dirt in others; ahead, the puddled roadbed mirrored a cold gray sky, then disappeared into the mist-shrouded valley, such that his way home appeared to float in a void. *So much for a bright future…*

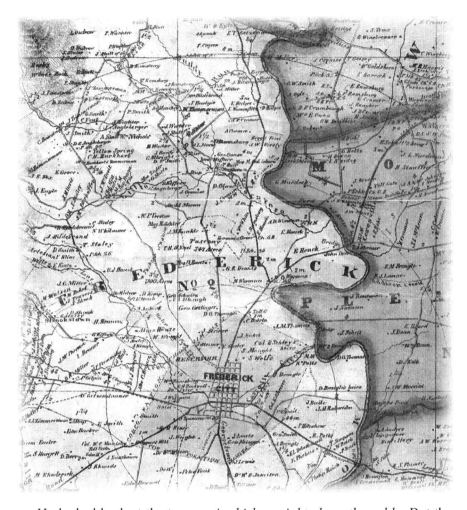

He looked back at the tavern. *A whiskey might chase the cold...* But the building showed no signs of life. It was then he noticed two figures watching him from the shadows of the crooked porch. One man was older, perhaps sixty. The pate of long, scraggly white hair that poked out from his wide-brimmed hat seemed at odds with the stiff black suit he wore. The other looked to be in his teens, and wore a butternut coat typical of many in the Confederate Army. An old bandage swathed much of his head, so that only one eye and the bottom of his face were visible; a gray kepi sat perched at an odd angle on top of the wrap. Under the bandage, the youth gazed

142

toward Spencer with his one eye and smirked. Both sat quietly in the cold, leaning back in chairs against the front of the canted structure, such that whole scene looked to be held up by the tavern.

"Tavern's closed, Yank. 'Tis Sunday. We observe the Sabbath."

Spencer realized he had no idea what day it was. He nodded at the man, "Right. Thanks." He gathered Tobey's reins, ready to mount.

"Ye lost?" asked the elder.

Spencer shook his head, "Ah, no. But thanks anyway." He had been warned to be cautious: passions ran high in areas where men served both armies. He had no desire to get involved in a conversation, much less with Rebels.

"Where ye headed?"

Dammit... Spencer turned around. The old man now stood, his lean, straight stature in disagreement with the slanted porch. The youth still sat against the building, staring with the same gap-toothed grin. Spencer didn't sense a threat; he felt uneasy all the same.

"Pennsylvania. Headed home."

"Goin' home, eh?" He studied Spencer, then said, "Ye look to be in one piece. Yer lucky." The old man took off his hat and scratched the back of his head, then smoothed the few white strands there; as he did, he gazed past Spencer at the mountainside.

"War took both my boys. Yankee shell hit both of 'em at once over at Sharpsburg. One fell swoop, as they say. Oldest boy died right off, I hear. I gather he's buried over there somewheres – his ma and I looked, but we couldn' find him."

"Mma-aaaah," the youth keened without moving an inch.

The man looked down at his hat, studying the inside. He tipped his head slightly back at the boy. "My youngest here caught a piece of it in the head. Went in one side and out the other; Doc doesn't know why he lived. Took a good part of him with it, I guess. Eats, sleeps; otherwise, he's pretty much like this, day in, day out. Anyways, 'least his ma got him home."

Spencer peered into the shadows; he realized the boy was actually gazing into the distance, seemingly grinning at nothing but the mountain. *Poor son of a bitch...*

"I was wounded at Antietam," Spencer said, "It was hell for both armies."

"They's different kinds of hell." The old man looked back at the mountain. "When that was all goin' on, we could hear the guns over here," he said quietly. "Sat right here wishin' I was with my boys. Don't know what I would've done, but wished I was there jes' the same." He stared at the mountain for a moment, then looked at Spencer, "T'was hell here too."

The old man replaced his hat and returned to his chair beside his son. "Ye want a drink, there's a hotel up the road a bit," he said, "But you got family waitin' on ye? Get on home, Yank. Get home."

Spencer nodded, "Obliged." He mounted, touched the brim of his hat in goodbye and spurred Tobey up the road, thankful to be leaving the place. On the porch behind him, the old man and his son still leaned against the wall. Both stared into the distance, but only the boy smiled.

The lowering sun appeared from behind the high cloud, and briefly warmed the road north. Spencer followed the turnpike past the shadowed farms tucked into the hollows that scalloped the mountainside. As evening fell, Spencer reached Mechanicstown; here, the next pass cut the Catoctins, and gave rise to another busy crossroads. By the tannery and shed rows at the edge of town, stood an aged wooden sign; in the fading light, he could just make out the lettering: Penna 20M.

Twenty miles, he thought. Almost home...

Spencer tethered Tobey outside a large stable, and rapped on the door until a squat man poked his head out of the small home next door.

"Yas?"

"Hello. Looking to put my animal up for the night."

"Right there."

The man closed the door behind him and waddled over to the stable door with a lantern. By his still-sooted shirt, and dark hands, Spencer took him to be the farrier. The man started to unlatch the barn and spoke excitedly and at length.

"Phew! Busy evening! Hear now," he said, "I take no Confederate scrip, just greenbacks. Now, I do lean toward the Secesh, mind you, but don't set

much by their money. What you got?"

His patience gone, Spencer looked down at his uniform and then glowered back at the proprietor. "Well shit, mister, I'll let you guess." He leaned toward the smithy, his hand resting on the Colt. "Can you take the animal or not?"

The blacksmith stepped back, his hands up, "Now, now, don't get yerself in a pucker there, Cap. I was jest goin' on. Wife says I don't know when to shet up. Guess she's right. 'Course I'll care for the animal."

Spencer started to unstrap his gear. "This horse has come a long road and needs good care. I'll pay extra." Again, Spencer leaned close to the man, "In greenbacks."

The man's head was already bobbing up and down. "Worry not, there, Cap. I am partial to horses regardless of they's affiliation. He'll be good as new in the morning." He looked at Tobey's scars, frowned, and peered up at Spencer. "Well, maybe a mite short of new; a long road, indeed."

Spencer paid the blacksmith, and hefted his pack and bedding up the road to the several large buildings that formed the town square. Despite the remoteness of the village, the hotel there was bustling: civilians, wounded soldiers on leave, those having business with the war, and others just as determined to get away from it.

Shuffling papers at the hotel's front desk stood a mustachioed clerk, his horn rimmed glasses perched on the end of his nose. Spencer waited a moment to let him finish his work, but without looking up, the clerk said coldly, "No rooms tonight. We're full up."

Spencer was growing cross with this bleak border state and its random mix of sympathies; he glared at the clerk. "No rooms for anyone, or just Yankees?"

Now the clerk peered up over his glasses, suddenly aware of this stranger's demeanor, and changed his tone. "Sir, we are loyal to the Union here, well, most anyway. I'm sorry, Captain, there are no rooms for anyone."

Spencer stared at the countertop. "Apologies, friend, it's been a long trip. Anyplace I can get something to eat."

"I can still get you dinner if you wish, sir," the clerk said, "And there may be a seat in the saloon."

"That would be fine. Obliged."

Spencer carried his bags into the bar and took a seat on one of the tall-backed benches that flanked the fireplace. The dinner the desk clerk ordered up was a bland stew with bread, but it was hot and filling; it would do. As dessert, he downed two glasses of whiskey and leaned back on the bench; the whiskey's warmth settled him. *Get on home, Yank...* He wrapped himself in his blankets and slept like the dead.

In the gray predawn, the dreams had come again; once again, their aftermath left him struggling, uncertain as to their reality. The first always began with Daniel approaching his front porch and tethering Tobey to the tie rail. Above, the front door opens and Sarah steps out; she wears a sunny blue dress that mirrored eyes welling with tears. She runs down the steps and holds him tightly.

"Welcome home, Daniel. Look who's here…"

The front door opens behind Sarah, and Luke's wife Anna steps out onto the porch. In her arms is a little girl: Daniel and Sarah's daughter. Mattie had grown so, he notes, with bright blue eyes like her mother. Smiling broadly, Anna passes the child to Sarah, who holds her up to Daniel. The little girl looks blankly at him. He hears a whispered,

"Who are you…?"

Anguished, he turns away and finds himself walking at night through an old forest – he guesses as much by the tang of dried sap and rotting wood;

the trees themselves show only as blurry shadows amid a glowing amber fog illuminated by flames visible just ahead. There, a ring of dark figures surrounds a campfire, but one seat remains at the edge in front of him. In the brilliant glow, the captain can't quite make out any faces, yet he feels welcome. He sits down and as his eyes adjust, he finds that those around him were indeed comrades – at one time: bleeding from their death wounds, here sit all those who died under his command, motionless, but staring at him, lifeless pupils wide and black. Then the flames in front the captain begin to grow higher and higher, the heat unbearable; he cannot move a muscle.

Spencer awakened with a start, and sat up in the booth clumsily, part of his body still asleep, tingling from the night on the hard wood, the other part half-scorched from the freshly stoked fireplace. He rubbed his face and looked about. Others, yawning and stretching, were starting to file in for breakfast.

He managed the hotel's spare meal of cold ham, biscuit, and coffee, then carried his gear to the stables. Tobey turned and nickered softly as Spencer entered the stable. As promised, the smithy had fed and groomed the animal; despite the long trip, Spencer noted that the horse looked healthier and more spry, as if sensing each step brought him further from a slaughterhouse corral.

The sun was rising just as he left Mechanicstown. Above the village, the mountain turned east, rising before him like a great brown wave in the chill morning mist. Further on, and just as abruptly, the height fell to a series of low ridges and hills as it rolled north. By mid-morning, Spencer had reached the head of the valley. The day was brighter, the air cool, but dry, and he was finally seeing familiar ground. He stopped on a rise south of Emmitsburg, just below the Mason-Dixon Line. There, the Catoctin rise ended, and farther to the west, the low range known as South Mountain rose into view; on its slopes lay Spencer's farm. *Home...*

Ahead, in the town's quaint square of frame houses and church spires, the way to Pennsylvania forked: one path led north to the crossroads village of Gettysburg; it lay in the valley only some ten miles east of Spencer's farm. To the left, a smaller road led west to the foot of the mountain at Fairfield; from there the road turned north to his home. After a year of his life with decisions in someone else's hands, he found the choice of routes began to nag at him.

The path through Gettysburg was more than another way home. In the early days of the war, Spencer had spent much time courting a young woman who taught there. Eventually, their bond ran its course and he would come to marry her sister: Sarah. *But there was a time...* And he occasionally found his thoughts lingering – and somewhat unsettled – over the decision.

In the end, the answer was straightforward enough. A foreseeable future may not returned to his prospect yet, but his past choices were clear. What he needed, the memory that had sustained him through nightmarish days and restless nights, was a return to his family, the home he knew, and attempt to restore what war had taken from him. *My life...*

He crossed the Emmitsburg square and turned west toward the Fairfield Road. Ahead lay the ridges and foothills of South Mountain; compared to the great rise of the Blue Ridge in Virginia, this was a height more broad than high; after all, he thought, more impressive looking down from than up to. *But it is home...*

By mid-afternoon, the late winter sun had dropped behind the mountain, spreading long, cold shadows in the vale road leading to the Spencer farm. The temperature dropped and Spencer shuddered, pulling the collar of his coat higher on his neck. Where the road began to steepen, he turned off onto the lane that led to his farm, and the images from the past came quickly. *This was my home. I remember these places. By those hickories there, Sarah and I watched the sunrise together. Sarah tried to plant lilacs over here...*

Spencer rode past the stand of large oaks at the edge of the lane and stopped; something felt *wrong*. It had been a year; surely it would take some time to adjust to a life without war, but there was something else missing. Riding up the lane, he could see the barn just ahead, the broad yard in front; up the slope beyond, their snug home of tan and gray fieldstone came into view. *And...?*

He had expected a wave of relief, some sense of finality; yet, he felt remote from this place, distant, a lack of feeling that went far beyond the wet March chill. The emotion was familiar enough: he had become skilled at isolating himself from his surroundings – but he wasn't expecting it here. Now, even as he rode up the lane, part of him began to withdraw into some dark corner of his being. *Stop this*, he thought, *you're home...*

Around the side of the house, a tall black man came into view, hammering a post in the rail fence that bordered the yard. He looked up frowning, but abruptly a broad smile crossed his face.

"Sakes alive...is that the Cap'n Spencer we heard tell of? Word had it you might be on your way; half expected it would be a week or two though. Good to see you!"

"No more than it is to see you, Lucius. How are you? How's Anna?"

"We're fine, we're fine. Anna's inside with someone I 'spect can't wait to see you."

Approaching the porch that bordered the front of the house, Daniel tried to shake off the moment's dreamy quality. He tethered Tobey to the tie rail. Above, the front door opened and Sarah stepped out, slowly at first, her mouth slightly parted in surprise; she wore a sunny blue dress that mirrored eyes welling with tears.

"Daniel!" Sarah ran down the steps and wrapped herself around him, kissing him long and hard, but realizing they weren't alone, pulled back, her face flushed. She smiled shyly.

"I've waited for so long... Welcome home."

"It's hard to believe I'm standing here," Daniel whispered; he breathed in the delicate scent of her. *Yes. Very hard to believe...*

As in his dream, the front door opened behind Sarah, and Luke's wife Anna stepped out onto the porch; he knew the truth of the moment, but his heart ached when he saw no child in Anna's arms.

Luke had walked up and joined Anna on the porch. "Hope we have something special for dinner. Looking like this fellow hasn't had home cooking in an age." Their laughs echoed in Daniel's ears.

Spencer stood, rooted at the foot of the steps. He looked from Sarah's smile, then to Anna and Luke on the porch above. They all looked so delighted. They all looked like strangers. The tableau on the porch slowly receded before him. Despite his long wait for this homecoming, he felt no closer to these people, or connected to his life here, than if he was reading a book. *A book about someone else...*

The journey home was going to take more time.

July 6, 1863: Night
Gettysburg

The moon rose over the town behind a thin pall of cloud: a short week past full and hued like pale rust, but large and bright enough to give dim outline to the wood and brick homes he passed. Lamps and candles still glowed inside several windows. The rain had long since stopped, even still, many of the sashes lay closed against the rank air.

Daniel turned onto the dark cross street he had followed earlier. A scattershot of thoughts now crossed his mind about the battle; lingering questions about what had happened, what might have been different. Corcoran's words rang in his ears: *There's nothing you could have done...* Daniel frowned at the notion.

He turned again onto High Street where the church and the Myers house stood. Ahead the area outside St. Francis was calmer now, but torches still burned there, casting long shadows up the road; Becky sat at the dark edge of one, silhouetted on the front step of the house. Daniel rode up slowly.

"Rebecca? Good Lord. I'm surprised you're still awake."

"I am, barely; but I said I'd wait for you. I just left your Sergeant. He woke up in a good amount of pain, but I gave him more laudanum. I think he'll sleep through the night. How's your other friend? Did you find what you what you wanted to know?"

Daniel tied Tobey to the post, and leaned on the railing beside the step, thinking. *She will never understand...* He started to recount his conversation with Corcoran, when Rebecca held her hand up to stop him. She thought for a moment, then looked up.

"That's it… Daniel. You're talking as if you're sorry you weren't right here with them. Is that what's been bothering you? You wish you had been there? That's it, isn't it?"

"Becky…" He stopped. *Perhaps she does understand…*

"Something tells me you'd be happier if you were lying inside like Sergeant Quinn…" Rebecca looked away, "Never mind. You don't have to answer; I know how you think." She sat for a moment in silence.

Calmer, she spoke quietly, "Daniel… I'm sorry." She stood and looked at him, her hands on his arm, fingers gently pressing the underside. She sighed, "I'm sorry. You came all the way down here to find me, and…" Then she looked away and shook her head. "We won't do this now. Look, it's no excuse for what I said, but I'm beyond tired. We both need sleep. You can stay here; the Myers have kept a room for me upstairs. You can put your horse in the stable out back; plenty of room now: the Myers' animals were taken by the Rebels. Go on back – I'll meet you in a few."

Daniel started to protest; she was gone before he had a word in edgewise. *And then there's Rebecca…* He untied Tobey and led him back to the small plank and batten building that stood behind the house. Putting a match to the lantern that hung beside the door, he looked inside: two stalls took up one side of the interior, the other side lay a matted pile of bloody clothes and hay; otherwise, the shed was empty. Daniel replaced the lamp on the peg, and in the dim light, raked the soiled straw and rags outside, then pulled fresh straw from the shallow loft overhead. He unsaddled Tobey and brushed him down while the horse nickered quietly.

"Long day, eh old man?" Daniel said, "I am pretty used up too. I think we'll do just fine out here." He walked to the door and gazed at the lamplight glowing inside the house. Rebecca. *What do you do about Rebecca?*

He said aloud: "You don't make things any more complicated…"

Daniel stepped back inside and pulled more straw from the loft, and made a second pile against the opposite wall; he spread his blanket over the top, sat down with a yawn and stretched out his legs. He closed his eyes and went over the day. *This will do just fine...* He pulled off his boots, and found himself weighing Corcoran's words again: *There's nothing you could have done...*

There was a soft noise outside. "Daniel?"

He looked up. Exhausted as he was, the image before him stirred something in the back of his memory: Rebecca stood framed in the doorway, now wearing a nightgown and a long shawl. *Lovely...* The setting moon behind gave a soft glow to the hair that now lay brushed to her shoulders – and also silhouetted the lissome figure under the gown. *Rebecca...*

She took the lantern from its peg and lifted it. "Daniel? Are you here?"

"Yes, over here..."

"There you are; I was beginning to worry..." In the wavering light, she noticed the blanket laid out on the straw. "I thought you were going to come inside?"

"Figured I'd bed down out here." He sat up and cleared his throat. "Air is not too bad out now. I can manage here, Becky."

He nodded at her attire, "Should the teacher be out wandering about like that?"

Rebecca shrugged. "It's late. And I rather think these are unusual circumstances." She sighed and studied him a moment.

"Look, Daniel. We're both exhausted, and maybe it's not the best time to bring it up..." She placed the lamp on the ground and spread the shawl on the fresh straw. "But there is something needs said; I don't know when we'll be alone again." She sat with her legs tucked beneath her, thinking out her words.

Daniel folded his arms across his chest and watched her in the lamplight. *Oh hell, here it comes...* He closed his eyes. He felt drained and his head throbbed. "Becky...let's not do this now."

"I'll make this as simple as possible. Lord knows we have enough to deal with." She leaned forward and looked in his face. "I know you and my sister have been through alot, Daniel; but I feel something else is wrong," she said quietly, "I just don't want that something to be me." Then she sat back, her lips pressed tightly, measuring her words carefully.

"It's this: I'm not sure how I'm supposed to act now. Sarah is my sister. When you married her, I was happy for you both. But I had to be…" She looked at him again, "Remember," she said, "I agreed we should part ways, but it wasn't…"

She looked away with her eyes starting to fill. Then she laughed softly to herself, "Good Lord, what's all this? More tired than I thought; maybe you are right. I best go."

He looked at her in the lamplight, shaking his head. "Becky, wait... I'm sorry. I haven't said anything because... It's not anything you've done. I don't know how to explain. Since I came home, nothing has felt right. Everything is different – and I don't fit. Poor Sarah, she's tried; but it's not something she can fix. It's all…changed. Now, with the Rebels right here, there have been dreams – nightmares. It all started me wondering…"

She nodded, watching him. "Go on…"

"Yes, your family asking me to find you safe was important," he said quietly, "But when I knew my regiment likely fought here, I knew I had to come; find out what happened." Daniel turned to her, "But if I hadn't found you, I don't know what I would have done."

He noticed a change in her expression as he talked, a quiet resignation in her eyes; she started to lean closer, but paused, unsure of herself. Before him, the top of her gown fell open and the lamplight spilled through the material and onto the gentle slope of her breast. *And then there's Rebecca…*

Daniel felt his breath rise, and they both bent forward to seal the decision. They kissed, undecided at first; soft, but compelling. He ran his hand over the curve of her hip, she moved to meet him with a quiet moan. At the same moment, the two pulled apart.

Rebecca's face reddened and she held her hand to her mouth, looking away. "Oh my God, I'm sorry. I don't know what I was thinking." She unconsciously clasped the top of her gown, and said softly, "I'm not sure what to think any more – other than we shouldn't do anything we need to feel guilty about."

Daniel cleared his throat and sat up, surprised by his lack of control, more so by the emotion it bared. "Don't be sorry," he said, "I guess there's more unsettled here than either of us thought…"

Rebecca sat back, then quickly folded her arms across her breasts where they pressed against the gown. "I'd say…" She self-consciously gathered up the shawl and wrapped it around her shoulders. Then they sat facing each other silently.

"But I am sorry, Daniel. I don't want to do anything to hurt you and Sarah. I can't imagine what I was thinking. I teach children here; I have a reputation to keep." She noticed his bemused gaze and frowned. "Get that out of your mind. No one knows about us here."

She put her hand atop his. "But at least we understand each other." She yawned. "Sorry – I really do need to sleep."

"Time we both got some rest," he said, "Maybe it is best I stay here, Becky. Like you said – nothing we have to feel guilty about. We can talk more in the morning."

She nodded and stood, brushing the straw from her gown. She was quiet as he walked her to the back door of the house. She turned, "There's nothing we really need to discuss in the morning, Dan. We understand each other just fine. Good night." She squeezed his hand and kissed him quickly, then she was gone.

July 7, 1863: Morning
Gettysburg

The sun's first rays reached the top of the church's bell tower, warming the shingles soaked by the predawn rain. In the stable below, Tobey nickered and scratched the floor of the stall with his hoof. Roused from the untroubled sleep of exhaustion, Daniel sat up and groaned; the old wound in his side ached from the day before, but the dull pain in his forehead had faded. He rubbed his eyes and looked around. Tobey put his head over the side of the stall and blew.

"Alright horse. I hear you, dammit, I hear you."

Daniel stood and stretched. He unhooked his grain sack from the oak upright, and gave Tobey a measure. He patted the animal's flank.

"I know you're hungry; we'll try to get you something fresh today, old man."

Daniel walked to the barn door and looked into the yard. He rubbed his face to wake up; despite the dull pain in his ribs, all in all, he felt rested. It came to him: since reaching the town, he had felt little of the isolation, the crippling memories that plagued his days at home. *This is the first place I've felt right in a long time: in the middle of this nightmare...* Odd, he thought. *Maybe the only place I fit in now is here...*

The sun was rising on a cool morning. It had rained again and the ground was wet and the air humid. The air was still rank, but the smell of strong coffee cut through, coming from the Myers' kitchen. Daniel rolled up his blankets and pulled his shirt on; raking his fingers through his hair, he walked to the back of the house. The door stood open and a dark-haired girl of seventeen or so stood just inside, her apron covered with flour. She fanned her hands over her face, and brushed the flour from her front, all the while gazing curiously at Daniel. She stepped outside.

"Well, hello! Whew! Hot in there!" She said excitedly. "You must be Captain Spencer. I'm Susan Myers. You met my sister yesterday."

Daniel smiled at her enthusiasm. "Yes I am, and yes I did."

"I thought so. No offense, but you're looking a tad worn. We just got a sack of coffee from Harrisburg – think we can spare you a cup; want some fresh?"

He smiled, "Sure. Thanks."

Daniel stepped inside; the kitchen was the same bustle of activity as the day previous. Another woman stood at the bake oven; she turned and studied him quickly, but said nothing. By her dark eyes and hair, Daniel guessed her to be the girl's mother; she looked exhausted. *Likely been up all night...* The Myers girl returned with a steaming tin of coffee. Daniel nodded thanks to her and took quick sips at the hot liquid. He hadn't tasted fresh coffee in a week.

"I think my sister and your Miss Wagaman are up the hall. You want, you can put your bags over there. They'll be safe."

Wonder if she even slept... Daniel dropped his bedding behind the door, excused himself and walked up the hall to the dining room where he had left Quinn. Sallie Myers was there; she knelt wiping the floor down where one of the badly wounded lay the day before. She looked at him, her eyes sad and tired yet.

"Morning, Captain Spencer." She nodded toward the sergeant. "Some good news, I think. You'll find your friend awake."

"Good morning, and thank you." Daniel looked past her. Quinn lay under the window; his head propped up on a rolled blanket, still deathly pale, but his eyes were open and clearer. He balanced a tin of the coffee in his good hand.

"Hello Cap'n. Have ya found that single malt yet?"

"Some things don't change; Quinn, you're a menace." Daniel knelt beside him. "And no; still no whiskey. Other than that, how you getting on?"

"Wellsir. Damn odd: the arm's surely gone, but I can still feel it – smarts some. But thankee fer askin'. Sure beats laying out on there in the damn rain, I tell you." Quinn coughed thickly; wincing, he took a sip of the coffee and lay back. He shifted about uneasily, trying to find a good position for the bandaged stump. He winced again, "Keep looking to lean on that elbow. Not havin' much success, a'course." He cackled weakly.

Spencer shook his head. "Lay easy, Sergeant."

"I thought I heard your voice," Rebecca walked in the room and knelt beside Daniel, laying her hand on his forearm. "I've been speaking with your Sergeant here; he is quite the charmer."

Quinn winked at her with a slight smile, but then shuddered, closed his eyes and stretched out. Rebecca nodded towards the door; they both rose and returned to the hallway.

"His fever is lower, I think." she whispered, "He's eaten some anyway, and we gave him something for the pain, so he should sleep."

"He looks a little better, I guess. You on the other hand…" Daniel frowned at the dark circles under her eyes. "Tell me you've gotten some rest?"

"Yes, I did; about three hours anyway, I was too wound up to get much more." She gave him a quick sidelong glance and then turned to go up the hall to the kitchen. "If you have time, I could use a hand with the food."

Daniel followed her, but stood in the kitchen doorway, staying out of Mrs. Myers' way. "I'll wait right here."

Across the room, the older woman still labored, now stirring a large pot of soup. Rebecca stood beside her, and spoke quietly, "Sakes alive, Mrs. Myers, please go lay down; you need to rest. I can do this."

The dark-haired woman turned; she looked exhausted, and tears ringed her eyes, "Not yet, not yet. I need to finish here. And we need more bowls, or cups, or something. To put soup in... All of my china is...well, I don't know what!" She waved her hands as if to ward off any further problems, and returned to stirring the large pot.

Sallie appeared in the doorway beside Daniel, watching her mother work feverishly. She spoke quietly, "Good Lord. She won't stop; she's been up most of the night. I'll give her 'til she finishes the soup and then I'm finding Father; he'll make her get some rest."

She turned to Daniel. "But she's right. Most of our bowls and such are up to the church. There looks to be alot of supplies arriving up the street now. Captain, think you can use your influence and find us something for the soup? And maybe some bandages, medicine, anything...?"

Daniel nodded, "Not sure how much influence I have these days, but I'll do my best." He turned to Rebecca who was still trying to help Sallie's mother. "I'll get what I can and then I'll be back to help you." He walked back up the hallway and out the front door.

The turmoil in the street outside the church showed no sign of letting up. Beside the roadway, the major that Daniel spoke with the previous day stood by a stack of crates, sorting through the large sheaf of papers that lay atop the boxes.

"Morning Major. How you making out?"

The officer nodded his head, still searching the pages. "Shipping inventory. Now there's a joke. Train wreck: that's more like it. I just about get one pile sorted out and then ten other things pile on top. No organization t'all." He looked at Spencer.

"Yes? What's your story?' the major squinted. "Now wait. Let's see – looking for a friend, right? Any luck?'

"Yes, I found him, thanks. A family up the street is caring for him. I could use your help again, sir; this family has taken in several wounded and could use a few things: cups, bowls, bandages, whatever you could spare."

"Not sure as I can *spare* anything." The officer eyed Spencer a moment, then said, "Check those boxes over there, find what you need and take it. A box or two short in this mess won't make one damn bit of difference. Just put it to good use." The major waved to a soldier that stood guard over another large stack of crates beside the church, and pointing to Daniel, he nodded approval. The soldier nodded back and saluted.

"Thank you Major." Spencer threaded his way through the chaos to the stack of crates. The guard, not much more than a boy, nodded to him; the youth's uniform was still crisp and showed creases, and the bluing on the rifle barrel he cradled showed it to be brand new. *Militia...*

"Morning, private. I'll be picking up some things for the wounded down the street."

The guard pointed behind the stack. "Yessir. If it helps, they's a couple of boxes already open over there." In fact, several already lay empty as their contents were quickly put to use.

"Thanks, private." He picked up an empty crate, and went from box to box, gathering bandages, laudanum, tin cups, and saucers – anything that might be of use for the injured at the Myers home. One stack of cases held bottles of brandy packed in straw. *Not Quinn's Irish whiskey, but it will do...* He pulled out two bottles and placed them in the box with the rest of the supplies, and stacked a pile of blankets atop the crate. Nodding thanks to the Major, he hefted the now bulky load back to the Myers house and made his way around to the back door.

Inside, the kitchen stood empty now, and quiet except for the hiss of boiling water spilling over onto the hearth. Daniel set the crate on the kitchen floor and retraced his steps back to the hallway. Rebecca stood in the dining room doorway. "The Sergeant's still asleep." She nodded toward the pallet where Quinn lay, his face twitched, but he snored deeply. She turned to Daniel.

"Sallie is putting her mother to bed; the woman is plain exhausted. I'm hoping Sallie gets some rest too." Rebecca looked away for a moment, uncertain, and then back at him. "I don't know what your plans are today. I'm sure Sarah is waiting for you at home. But if you could stay a little longer and help us, there's so much to do."

Daniel nodded. "Of course I'll help. Sarah knew I'd be gone a couple of days. And I need to figure out what to do about the sergeant. I can't leave him like this..."

"Good." Her eyes softened, relieved for a moment, but then she turned quickly, walking quickly back to the kitchen, "Let's go. While Mrs. Myers is resting, you can help me get some soup into these boys. Then when Sallie has rested, we'll go up to the church."

There were but nine or ten wounded in the close rooms of the home, but their care took most of the morning. Rebecca and Daniel went from injured man to injured man with bowls of the hot broth, replacing old dressings, and perhaps just as important to those suffering far from home: offering a few words of comfort. By midday, they had done all they could. Sallie and her mother were both awake and once again in the kitchen, so Daniel and Rebecca left for the church.

The hospital there had grown more crowded still. It was clear that family members of some of the injured had started to arrive, and several now walked the aisles, searching, their faces a mixture of desperate compassion and stunned horror. To the side of one aisle sat a middle-aged woman in an elegant green dress; beside her lay a figure, an officer's coat covering his head and shoulders. Other than the reddened skin where tears had streaked her cheeks, the woman's face was pale as death. She rocked slightly, her hands covering her ears against the horrid sounds around her. Rebecca took the woman's hands gently in hers, and embraced her until an attendant arrived.

For the rest of the afternoon, they tended to those who, despite torn body and anguished spirit, had managed to survive another day. Daniel listened to those who wanted to talk, offered encouragement to those who could only listen. He found little anger toward their foe, as though all of war's vitriol had drained from them with the lifeblood they left on the field. But in the end, he half thought all his efforts futile: no amount of care or healing skills could make headway in such a tide of suffering. The thought rose again: *Why did I survive?*

The sun was long set when Daniel and Rebecca finally left the church; Becky walked beside him, her gaze fixed, saying nothing. On reaching the Myers' threshold, Sallie met them in the hallway; she appeared exhausted still. She took Rebecca aside and they quietly discussed the condition of the wounded in their care.

Daniel excused himself. "Be right back, I'm going to check on my horse."

Sallie turned to him wearily. "Oh, Captain Spencer, I almost forgot: that boy Elliot must have taken a liking to your animal, he actually came by and asked if he could feed and water him. Some trials bring out the best in people."

Daniel smiled. *Some trials and another dollar...* "Well, I'll have to thank him. I'll just make sure the horse is set for the night." He made his way to the barn, and to his amazement, not only found Tobey fed, but his trough full and the stall mucked out. *I'll be damned; maybe there's some hope for the boy after all...*

Returning to the house, he found Rebecca in the dining room with Quinn. She sat on a low stool, changing the sergeant's dressing by lamplight; the two talked quietly. The sergeant seemed awake and more animated – and one of the bottles of brandy stood on the floor beside him. He noticed Daniel standing in the doorway.

"Now there you are," Quinn said, "Glad to see you Cap'n." He rubbed the whiskers under his chin and cackled, "For that matter, glad to see anything 't'all." He coughed for the effort.

Spencer nodded toward the bottle. "Well, Sergeant, I see you've decided to give up on Irish remedies."

"Not hardly," Quinn winked, "But this brandy here's a damn sight better than the popskull we had in camp. Any port in a storm, Cap'n."

Rebecca stood up and shrugged, "Wasn't my idea, the sergeant was in some pain – but he seemed more interested in a drink than the laudanum." She turned down the oil lamp, and gathering up the basket of dressings, walked to the door. She looked quickly at Daniel, but her eyes didn't meet his.

He took her hand, "Are you alright?"

"I'll be fine. Just… I just have to check on some of the others. I'll leave you two to talk."

Daniel watched as she disappeared down the dark hallway. There was something: her voice was impassive and her look distant. *Damn odd…* He pulled up the stool and sat beside Quinn.

"So, Sergeant, glad to see you again."

"Wellsir, same here. Last I saw you in February, I didn't think that was likely. Tell you what," Quinn wagged his good hand toward the bottle and metal cup beside it, "Let's have a drink and you can tell me what you've been up to. All considered, the brandy warms me chest better than that laudanum."

As Daniel poured some of the amber liquor into the tin, Quinn nodded his head at the brandy bottle. "Come now, Cap'n. Hate to drink alone."

Oh what the hell… Daniel handed the cup to Quinn, then lifted the bottle and took a long drink. He hadn't eaten since midday, and the liquor's tart warmth spread through him quickly. For the better part of the next hour, the two men caught up on what had passed since Fredericksburg. Then at the end, and at Daniel's prompting, the sergeant told what he remembered of the first day's battle, and his ordeal since.

"But I tell you, all things considered, I feel blessed to end up here," Quinn said almost to himself, then looked up. "And the young lady caring for me – your wife's sister? We been talkin' some. She tells me I might have you to thank for that."

Dammit, Becky… "Don't listen to all that Conall," he said, "I was lucky to find you. It was Sallie Myers that got you here," Daniel shook his head. "Now I think you best get some sleep."

Quinn wasn't finished. "Yessir. Lovely girl, she is. Seems to care about *you* a fair bit. Thinks you're not feeling quite so fortunate..." He tossed back the last brandy from the cup. "Ah, yessir, thas good. And, if I take her meaning, you been thinkin' you should have stayed in the army; that somehow you let the boys down by not being here with them? Now. With all due respect, sir, have you taken leave of your bloody senses? Do you not remember why you left?" Another deep cough rose in the sergeant's chest.

"You need to rest, Conall," Daniel cleared his throat and started to stand, "We can talk more tomorrow."

"We could at that," Quinn frowned, but then nodded toward the bottle again. "But that last nip did me wonders; b'fore you go, let's you and I have one more."

Daniel knelt down and poured more liquor in Quinn's cup, "Here's a bit more. but I'll save my drink for one of the wounded..."

Quinn sipped at the cup, gazing at him, "Cap'n? One way t'other, there's no one here who isn't wounded." He looked to Daniel, and nodded again at the brandy.

"Oh hell, Quinn..." Daniel took another pull and set the bottle down. "Of course I remember why I left. Alright? But seeing what happened here – to you, to Jim Corcoran – all these men? I shouldn't have left the regiment. I should have been here with you all; it might have made a difference."

"Cap'n. Nothin' you could do would change what happened that day."

Spencer shook his head, "Yes, Corcoran said the same. That's not how I feel..."

Quinn eyed him thoughtfully. "Laddie, you don't owe me or Corcoran or anyone else anythin'. You certainly don't owe this damn war anythin'. All you owe is to yourself: to get home, get on with things best way you can, and live the life the good Lord intended."

Daniel stared at the polished floor, thinking on Quinn's words. "Not sure if I can do that," he said quietly, "Being home is not what I expected. Everything is changed. I don't belong there."

"You don't understand, Cap'n," Quinn said, shaking his head. "A man can't wait to leave the damn war, but the damn war never leaves him. Doesn't seem like the same home you left, because you are not the same man who left – it's you that's changed."

Daniel thought on that. "Alright. Maybe I could live with that, but..." He stopped and looked up at Quinn, "Look, you once told me that getting through war is like climbing a mountain, some get to the top, some don't, and only look back. Well, shit, I didn't make it. And now all I can do is look back. Some small thing will remind me, and it's all there like I never left. So what's the difference?"

Quinn studied him again. "Yessir. A puzzle, it is," he added, "A man does his damndest to get home in one piece, then can't help but wonder if things wouldn't have been better if he kept gettin' shot at."

The sergeant took another gulp of brandy and stared out the window into the darkness, "Conall Quinn? Oh, he stayed; he was tomfool enough to reenlist." He winced and lay back, closing his eyes. "Looks like I stayed a mite too long..." He sighed, and looked back at Daniel, "But as I say, everyone takes a wound."

"And what about our boys that died," Daniel whispered, "What about them? I lived, and good men – better men than I – didn't."

The sergeant opened his eyes, trying to focus, then frowning to himself. "Better than you, you say. Who's to say whether a man is good or bad? B'sides – all that has nothing to do with it. It's a goddamn war. Devil or angel, terrible things happen no matter who you are."

He turned to Spencer. "Here now: with what I seen, faith's a little hard to hold on to. But trust me, Cap'n, if the Lord ever sat judgment on all this, he stopped when he saw what we've done to each other. No matter what some of them collars say, this is not God's will – there's no grand plan. Things just happen, and it's our lot to come up with reasons afterward."

Quinn downed the last of the cup, and looked back at Daniel blurrily, whispering, "Cap'n, leaving the war was the right thing to do." He reached across with his good hand and took Daniel's arm. "Laddie, now you need to get on with the rest of your life."

With that, the sergeant lay back and rasped a long sigh. "Sorry Cap'n," he whispered, "I think I'll be needing to rest my eyes for just a minute or two." His eyes closed, fluttered once or twice, then Quinn's breath deepened and he dozed off.

Daniel sat for a moment, watching his friend's chest rise and fall in the dim light. He corked the brandy bottle, stood and stretched the cramps from his legs. He walked with some difficulty down the dark hall to the kitchen. It was growing late, but the fire in the broad hearth still lit the room; the glowing heat made his head swim. What was it had Quinn said? *It's you that's changed...* Daniel placed the bottle on the long wooden table and leaned for a moment. When his eyes adjusted, he saw Rebecca sitting beside the hearth stirring stained linen in the boiling water. She turned and looked at him with sad eyes, then turned back to the fire, and said, "You look terrible. Are you alright?"

"Just tired. Quinn is asleep. Maybe I should do the same."

She stood and walked to the other side of the table and leaned with her head down. The lamplight barely colored a face pinched with exhaustion. "I'm about past tired," she said softly. She lifted the brandy bottle and held it up to the light. She looked at Daniel.

"My, it appears you and the Sergeant have been busy. And why not..." She found a small claret glass in the kitchen cabinet, filled it to the top. "Join me?"

"Ah, no. Think I've had enough; but you…well, go right ahead." He watched as she downed half the glass; he knew Becky was fiercely unconventional, but he smiled with surprise. "So the teacher drinks liquor?"

"Liquor? Not usually," She took another large swallow and made a face, "Brandy? Sometimes. Tonight, definitely."

She picked up the glass and returned to the hearth. Rebecca gazed blankly into the coals, and Daniel leaned on the table, silent as well, each keeping to their thoughts. It was some minutes before she spoke again. She started quietly, but her words belied her composure.

"Sorry, Mister Captain Spencer, I don't know how much more of this I can stomach. Been at this for five days; helping the doctors, bandaging what's left of these men, some died in spite of all I did. And there's just no end to it." Rebecca looked back at the fire and sipped the brandy, her voice a hoarse monotone now.

"Did you know they started burying them in a big trench across the street? But it rained so hard the other day that their bodies floated up. So the orderlies put planks on them to hold them down. Slabs of wood…" Rebecca looked at him, her face twisted with pain.

"No one should have to see things like that! No one..." She took another swallow and looked into the amber liquid.

"But, you know, I was alright, I was fine until up at the church this afternoon – I truly was. But there was this man…no, he was a boy. Hole in his stomach so big the surgeons couldn't even close it. I was just checking his dressings – horrible. And then he woke up. Thought I was his mother... Oh, he didn't last long, just held my hand and begged me to take him home." Tears streaming down her cheeks, Rebecca walked to the other side of the table and put the glass down. She looked at Daniel.

"Do you know what that does to a woman?"

Suddenly she slammed her hands on the oaken tabletop, crying, "No one should have to see things like this! No one! It's a nightmare there's no waking from…" Then she was still, staring at the tabletop and her reddening palms. "I'm sorry. But I need to know... Why does this happen? What am I supposed to do…?"

Daniel walked around the table and put his arms around her. Quinn was right. *There's no one here who isn't wounded…* Rebecca buried her face in his neck and sobbed repeatedly. *No one should have to see things like that...* Those that survived this meaningless horror would have to find their own way.

"Rebecca, you're not alone; I understand more than you realize," he whispered.

"I'm not alone? Really? After that boy today, I realized just how alone a person can be."

They held each other for some time. The sound of rain pelting the windows rose over the crackle of the hearth and sporadic groans from the front rooms. When Rebecca finally lifted her head to him, their eyes met in an open question, a moment vulnerable, uncertain. They both let it pass, but held each other in the firelight until she slowly turned away, taking a long, deep breath and letting it fade.

"Good Lord; I gotten myself all wound up," Rebecca wiped the tears from her cheeks and cleared her throat. "I'm sorry – I keep saying that, don't I?" She held her hands to her temples, and said, "And then there's you and I," she half-laughed, "I wonder sometimes…"

"Becky, please stop," Daniel said softly, "We've had enough for one day; we both need to rest. And the last question? You and I made that decision last night. The right one. Nothing is different tonight, except we're even more tired – and the brandy – which is good a reason as any not to change anything."

Tears still welling in her eyes, Rebecca brought a hand up to his cheek and tried to smile, "Thank you. As always, you're the voice of reason. I never should have let you go…" She finished the brandy, and set the glass solidly back on the table. "You always made me happy. But I was young, and I didn't need more than that then; you did. I wasn't surprised, or unhappy, when you fell in love with my sister."

"Rebecca…" Daniel sighed; Quinn's words rose at every turn. *You need to get on with the rest of your life…*

She wiped her eyes with her sleeve and picked up the lamp. "But since all that's settled now, come upstairs; no reason you can't sleep in a dry bed tonight, and I'll sleep in the chair. We'll leave my door open and if anyone thinks it's oh so indecent, they can take it up with me."

He stopped trying to reason any more. Daniel retrieved his packs from the corner, and followed her down the hall. They walked quietly up the stairs to a small bedroom at the rear of the house. Becky placed the lamp on the dresser and revealed a room warm and close, just fitting the dresser, trundle bed and a slipper chair. He sat heavily onto the bed that filled most of the room and pulled off his boots. He rubbed his eyes and he felt his head swim. When he looked up, Rebecca still stood beside the lamp; she had closed the door behind her and leaned her head back gazing at the ceiling.

"Yes, I closed the door. How improper of the teacher. But I need to shut all off that out for one night. Lie down and get some sleep now, Daniel Spencer. I'll be fine in the chair."

"Not a chance Becky," he said, "You need sleep too. I have my bedding right here. I'll be fine on the floor." Daniel unrolled his blankets beside the low bed, pulled off his shirt, lay back and closed his eyes. For a few moments, he listened to Becky moving, the rustle of dress and petticoats, and then the creak of the bedframe as she lay down. Then there was a quiet sobbing.

Daniel opened his eyes and sat up. The lamp now stood by the bedstead and its flicker, he could just make out Rebecca; she lay on her side in her shift, tears rolling silently down her cheeks.

"Becky..."

"I'll be fine Daniel. Please go to sleep..."

He climbed onto the bed, lay against her back, holding her as she sobbed until sleep cut her tears. *There's no one here who isn't wounded...*

July 8, 1863: Morning
Gettysburg

A faint glow and the sigh of rain came through the small window above. His eyelids opened heavy with sleep; it was early, and he felt like hell, but he wanted to be up and out before the house was awake. Daniel sat up groggily, and as he rose, an ache moved from one side of his head to the other. *The brandy...* Beside him, Rebecca drew the long breath of a deep slumber. *Let her sleep...*

He quietly pulled on his clothes, opened the door, and peered down the hall. Other than an occasional moan from one of the wounded, and the snore of the orderly sleeping by the stairs, all was quiet. He gathered up his blankets and boots, closed the door gently behind him, and made his way quietly down to the front door.

He sat under the small overhang that covered the front step, and drew a deep breath. The mist from the downpour wet his face, and the cool air was refreshing, but little relief for the dull pain in his forehead. *Damn. Brandy...what was I thinking.* He held his head trying to collect his thoughts. He set his boots between his feet and gazed down; it took a longer moment to sort which foot went where. Finally, he stood and walked slowly around to the barn in the wet predawn glow; rusty hinges creaked as he pulled the door closed.

Daniel leaned against the hand-hewn center beam that rose to the ceiling. Discounting all the thoughts that fought for resolution, he felt like hell, inside and out. *What was I thinking...* The ache pushed at the crown of his head, his mouth felt like singed hide, and tasted much the same. Over it all, bits and pieces of the previous night's conversations churned in his thoughts. *No one should have to see things like that... It's you that's changed...*

Mixed with the rundle of showers above, there was a quiet, wet sputter. In the far corner of the shed, he found that Mr. Myers had run a drainpipe into a small barrel to provide water for the stable. *Pennsylvania Dutch. Practical as hell...* Daniel pulled off his damp shirt, took a bucket and filled it from the runoff. At first, he cupped his hands, splashing the cool water over his face and his neck. *The hell with it...* On a cross beam above the barrel sat an old chunk of lye soap; he scrubbed himself, lifted the pail over his head and emptied it. He came up stunned and sputtering, but feeling days better. He shook himself dry and put on the change of clothes from his pack. He combed his hair back with his fingers. *Better. This will do...*

Tobey had watched him quietly from the stall, but now whinnied.

"Sorry old man. You're next." He filled the trough with the fresh water and gave the animal a measure of grain. He patted the horse's neck. "Heading home soon, Tobey. I'm not finished yet. I'll be back..." The cool water had shocked him awake, but did little to answer the questions that vied for resolution. Quinn's words again. *Things just happen, and it's our lot to come up with reasons afterward...* For a minute, he unconsciously dug through his saddlebags that lay on the railing. *What are you looking for?* He pressed at his temples. Tobey watched over the stall rail with his scarred eye.

In the end, Daniel untied his blanket from the cantle, wrapped it around his shoulders, and walked through the cloudburst to back door of the Myers' home. The door was closed, but unlocked; he stepped inside, the kitchen was warm and dry, and the air sweet with the smell of fresh bread and fried pork.

Sallie stood at the table, slicing a long loaf of bread. She looked up: her mouth still in taut grief, but on seeing him, her eyes softened, and her demeanor brightened some.

"There he is. Good morning, Captain. Did you get some rest?"

"Yes, slept a bit. Thanks. Hope you've managed some sleep too."

"A few hours, I think. Really had to. We were all running the string out too far; we can't do any good for these men that way. I think 'Becca is still upstairs. May I can get you some coffee awhile?"

"Certainly, I just want to check on Sergeant Quinn."

"Your friend is still asleep." Sallie nodded with a small frown toward the almost empty brandy bottle that still sat on the table. "Guess that might have helped some." She turned and brushed the flour from her apron.

"This morning they sent us some food, so today the boys will wake to a decent breakfast. A favor? They promised they'd have some salt and sugar if we came back. We could use it for this meal if you wouldn't mind. I'll have that coffee when you get back."

"Of course. I'll see what I can do." Daniel stepped back outside, relieved: the young woman's dark eyes asked much of him. *There's no one here who isn't wounded...* He draped the rubber blanket around his head and shoulders and made his way down the puddled street. Beside the church, a square quartermaster's tent now stood; inside, the gray-bearded major worked at a small table. As he entered, Daniel thought on their afternoon meeting in the street. *Not even two days ago...* Despite his still-harried appearance, the officer recognized Daniel, and quickly arranged for a package of salt and somewhat more sugar. Daniel thanked him and splashed back down the street with the parcels.

The sun had risen behind the clouds, but the showers came down in earnest, and the bright downpour blanched his view; up the road, he made out a figure sitting beneath the overhang that covered the Myers' front steps. *Becky...* She sat with the hem of her dress just skimming the water that ran at her feet, looking at her hands that lay together in her lap. As Daniel approached she looked up, her face drawn and the strands of hair at her temples already gone damp.

"Rebecca? Everything okay?"

"I'm fine." She smiled at him, then looked back at her hands. "Just need to say something here: last night I fell to pieces. I'm sorry. I said I didn't want to add to your problems and I have."

"Becky, it's fine. But maybe you should come back to the farm with me," Daniel whispered," Get away from all this..."

"No, Dan, I'm alright," she said, "Last night we both needed something – someone – that wasn't a part of all this pain. I glad we had each other. Now it's behind us. I'm fine." Rebecca was adamant as always: despite the bleak prospect remaining ahead, she would stay in Gettysburg. Here she could offer something meaningful in the midst of such aimless ruin.

Suddenly, Sallie appeared in the doorway behind Rebecca, wringing her hands in her apron. "Captain? 'Becca? I think you better come inside," she said quietly, "the Sergeant..." Rebecca looked at Daniel; her expression fell and she turned to follow Sallie back into the house.

No, not Quinn... Daniel stepped up the threshold, pulling off the wet slicker and dropping it on the railing. He stood beside Rebecca at the entrance to the dining room, leaning on the dark wood casing. The low rasp of Quinn's breathing rattled across the room. Sallie now knelt beside a medical orderly who was placing the back of his fingers to various spots on the sergeant's face and neck.

"...Fever's high, but I don't think it's from the wound; his breathing don't seem right. I'm no surgeon, M'am, but I'm guessing pneumonia. He was lying out there a long time. Even without the other injury to the man, I'd not set high hopes."

Sallie clasped her hand to the collar of her dress. "Please, we just lost another man yesterday. Not again. There must be something we can do..."

The attendant pulled his forage cap down over his head, and rose to leave. "Well, a city hospital might know what to do, but we're a long sight from that here. I gave him some opium and camphor, so he's comfortable. I'll be back. Maybe some cold plasters and calomel..."

Daniel had heard enough of the man's advice. "Get out."

"Hey mister, I'm just..."

Spencer now stood in the middle of the room, glowering at him, "Did you not hear me? Get the hell out."

The orderly shrugged, picked up his medical bag and gave Daniel wide passage as he left. Other than the rain pelting the windows and the sergeant's labored breath, the houseful of wounded stood oddly quiet. Daniel knelt down and felt Quinn's forehead. *God. Hot as an iron...*

Sallie, still kneeling silently beside him, cleared her throat. "What should we do? Maybe the orderly was right. Maybe there's something..."

"Shit," Spencer laughed, "These fools would give him calomel – that's mercury: that just makes you sicker. I've had their cures. I lived in spite of it. No, Quinn's tough; we make him comfortable and see what happens." He dropped his gaze to the polished floor.

"Well then, Captain, I will pray for him," Sallie said.

The idea only vexed Daniel more. *"With what I've seen, faith is a little hard to hold on to..."* He looked at her, but held his temper.

"Thank you," he said finally, and returned his gaze to Quinn.

Rebecca put her hand to Sallie's shoulder and nodded towards the door. "We're going to look in on some of the others." She said quietly, "I'll be back in a bit. I'm sorry, Daniel," and the two women left the room.

Quinn's breath rose noisily again and Daniel lay his hand his shoulder. "Lie easy, Conall" he said quietly, "You deserve better..."

"...terrible things happen no matter who yar..."

Daniel turned. *What the hell?* Across the room was another badly wounded man who had lain unconscious in his blanket for two days; he now muttered in some dream.

"...get on with your life..."

The effect of Quinn's words repeated by the comatose figure was unsettling. Daniel shook off the unease and sat down. He wrapped his arms around his knees, watching the gray rain pelt the room's tall windows.

As the morning wore on, warm air blew from the northeast, driving the towering rain clouds down and against South Mountain. Sarah sat beside the porch window as she had since first light, staring into the updraft of clouds that roiled up the slopes toward her; Gettysburg lay somewhere far back in this murk. Where was Daniel? Rebecca? What had happened, she wondered, was everything alright?

Anna walked up behind her and put a blanket over her shoulders; she glanced at the side of Sarah's face, and then peered out the window with a look that seemed to pierce the fog.

"Honey, just sit tight. Things take as long as they take – and the man has lots to sort out. There's nothing you can do'll change what happens there."

At the window's wet edge, a drop formed and ran slowly down to the sill.

July 8, 1863: Afternoon
Gettysburg

The rain stopped just before midday; Conall Quinn stopped breathing just after. It wasn't apparent right off: the commotion throughout the house continued as though nothing had changed; but the low rattle in his chest gradually slowed and went silent. Daniel covered the sergeant's face with the blanket and sat motionless beside him.

In time, he stood and walked to the kitchen. There, Mrs. Myers and her younger daughter still labored to prepare food for the injured. He stopped in the doorway and cleared his throat. "The sergeant in the next room has died," he said, "Don't let the orderlies take him. I will be making arrangements for the body."

Before the two women had time to react, Daniel had walked silently out the back door. *They put boards on them to hold them down...* He would take care of Quinn's burial now, not the Army. Just as important at that moment, he needed to move; get somewhere, anywhere that involved not being still, not dwelling on the feelings that vied for attention. He quickly saddled Tobey, and trotted out past the anguish at the church, turning south down the Baltimore Road.

The sun appeared from behind the clouds, and wet brick faces of the row houses glowed reddish-orange. The homes on this street showed the same somber disquiet, outside and in, as the other parts of town, but here it was plain there had been hard fighting. Most of the buildings were pocked with bullet holes and broken windowpanes. Where the road descended toward the edge of town, part of a Southern barricade of boxes and barrels still stood: cracks and splinters showed in the damp wood where Yankee lead sought softer landing.

Ahead, the turnpike rose again, climbing a long grade to Cemetery Hill, one of the higher prospects in the valley. On the hillside, pallid rows of tents marked a camp of militia, but beyond, save for a tall poplar and the cemetery's somberly painted gatehouse, the height was broad and open. Corcoran had told him this hill was where the Yanks retreated that first day, where they stopped and fought again, and it was here, he said, that the tables started to turn on Lee's army. Spencer turned Tobey from the road and urged him up toward the eastern crest.

For the moment, he found the spot somehow comforting: solitary, but expansive, a place that drew him beyond the clamor of his thoughts. Unlike the town, surrounded by dazed inhabitants, cheerless streets, and the small, close structures full of despair, here was a sweeping view. In the rain's aftermath, the vista before him was bright and clear, spreading down to the broad cluster of houses below, then to the tall cupolas marking the College and Seminary buildings, and beyond to the ridges and fields of battle around the town. Further to the west, he could see the tail of the lingering storm still drifting against the mountainside. The paler blue-green color of the vale where his farm lay made it seem all the more distant. *Sarah... Blue eyes in the dawn. Will we ever have that again?* On the bleak hilltop, the answer lay distant as well.

The ruin Spencer had ridden through west of town was random; here it was plain the ground had been used for ends more untoward. In its indifference, the rain had refreshed the scars of war as well. In the roadway, water puddled behind the remains of a stone breastwork that still lay on the rutted path. Federals had dismantled the proper wood fence that once framed the turnpike, its rails now stacked and mounded with great piles of earth to shelter cannon and artillerymen. The defenses had done little for the horses that drew the guns: several lay nearby in bloated heaps, harnessed even in death.

Even so, crossing the ruined hillside Daniel felt a familiarity with the place. Here, things almost made sense. *The only place I fit in...* For the uninitiated, the odd facing of the artillery defenses seemed haphazard; to Spencer, the purpose was clear: crossing fields of fire, long and short, covering the town and the open ground to the east. Anyone attacking this hill would be caught under a hail of iron. *Powerless...* He gazed down the eastern slope: fresh graves of wet, brown-black earth rowed the farmland below, and spoke of such an attempt; from their number, a failed attempt.

It all seemed so clear: across these fields, the lines of battle maneuvered; around these hills, the generals shifted their pieces in some deadly chess game. Spencer's gaze drifted back across the disfigured crest: on either side of the turnpike, the squat brick gatehouse and the tall poplar stood like the king and queen's piece. In the cemetery beyond, Gettysburg's distinguished and unremarkable alike were interred; now, regardless of stature, several of the granite stones lay in the mud like so many toppled bishops and pawns.

Yet no answers... Whatever had happened here, it was finished. The armies were gone; Quinn – and countless others – dead, the battle now a piece of the past that someone else would describe in glowing terms. All that remained now was the torn hilltop. *And this is only temporary, the ground does not scar forever, it doesn't remember us.*

At this thought, his focus melted away. He dazedly turned Tobey toward the road and let the animal thread his way through the muddy defenses. Amidst the ringing in his head, Spencer could hear the faint haft and chink of pick and shovel hitting rocky soil. *Militia digging more graves...*

He rode across the Pike, through the gatehouse, and found but two people digging at the ground: a woman and an elderly man. Both looked up as he approached: the woman held the brim of her faded bonnet against the glare, the old man frowned, wiped his forehead with his sleeve, and turned back to his labor. Around them, a number of wood stakes pinned the side of the slope into neat squares. *Burial plots...* Here was an answer: *I will bury Quinn here. Where at least something makes sense...*

Spencer dismounted and gazed over the staked ground. He pulled off his hat and turned to the woman. "M'am, my name is Spencer. I take it all these graves are for soldiers? Isn't the militia helping you?"

The woman leaned on the shovel, catching her breath. Mud caked the hem of the woman's dress, and perspiration stained the front and underarms. With a clipped German accent, the woman sighed, "Afternoon, Mister Spencer. No sir, des is town cemetery. Graves here are purchased private." With a deep intake of breath, she straightened up, and put her hand to the small of her back: the bodice showed her to be far along with child.

"My name is Thorn, Mr. Spencer... 'Lizbeth Thorn," she said. Her husband, she explained, was the caretaker of the cemetery, but was in the Union army; the maintenance of the cemetery grounds – and any burials – had now fallen to her. It was clear she and her father were only beginning their work.

"During da battle, ve go away down country. Yesterday ve get back." She nodded toward the gatehouse, "Our house is out of fix; full of hurt soldiers, blood and dirt... But now families pay to bury dere boys, and da graves must be dug by us."

She looked toward the gatehouse, then at the hole at her feet. "Don't know vere to start," she lifted the shovel and pushed it back into the dirt, "So, I start here." She stared down the row of plots and whispered distantly, "Yas, much to do..."

"M'am, I won't trouble you. But I would like to bury a friend here," Spencer said, "I will pay you, and I will dig the grave."

"Sorry for your friend. Yas, so many boys dead..." she said, studying him a moment. "No. You pay us, Mister Spencer, we make the grave for your friend. You come back later dis afternoon, it'll be done."

Spencer nodded thanks, mounted Tobey and trotted down the hill. *Now to find Elliot...* Turning up the street toward the hospital at St. Francis, he found the now customary buzz of activity outside, but sitting in almost the same spot across the road was the towheaded boy. Spencer called to him. The youth stood when he heard the voice.

"Yes, Captain? Want me to watch your horse?"

"No boy. This is more important." Spencer said, "And we'll need your father's wagon."

Later that afternoon, Daniel stood silently over Quinn's grave.

On his return to town, he had purchased the hastily made casket from one of the busy woodworkers on Baltimore Street, then hired Elliot's father to take the sergeant's remains to the cemetery. When the wagon was ready to leave, Rebecca and Sallie were still making their rounds of the wounded. *Just as well,* he had thought. It was one thing to watch a man breathe his last, quite another to watch him laid in the ground. Daniel left word for Becky on his leaving, and led the wagon up to the cemetery alone.

With the setting sun, a steady breeze blew in from the west; long amber beams skimmed the unfinished grain of the coffin lid. With the afternoon's rushed preparations, an odd sense of motion still lingered over the quiet moment. Mrs. Thorn and her father had stopped their work, and stood a ways off as caretakers will, waiting patiently. *There must be something I should do,* Daniel thought. *Some words...* Perhaps not; even were there a man of the cloth present, Quinn was not one for scripture. *"Faith is a little hard to hold on to..."* Anything more prosaic rang hollow to him. *Conall Quinn, your war is finally over...* Was there nothing else to say? Daniel's thoughts were scattered; nothing seemed to say enough. But on the breeze, he heard Quinn's own words rise and fall: *You don't owe me or anyone else anythin'... All you owe is to yourself...*

"Rest easy, Sergeant," he whispered. At that moment, Rebecca walked up beside him and took Daniel's arm. They stood together quietly for a time. Daniel turned and nodded to Mrs. Thorn. Minutes later, he helped them lower the coffin into the ground. While the last rays of sunset withdrew behind South Mountain, spadefuls of dirt dropped on yet another man's grave.

It was just dark enough to need a lantern when he led Tobey into the stable behind the Myers house. The anxious energy that had carried Daniel through the day was gone. He rubbed the animal down and tried to row up his thoughts, but as he tried, nothing seemed in focus. He knew it was time he headed home, but something still weighed on him.

Two days before, his purpose in coming to the town seemed clear enough. As it happened, he had been lucky: he had found Rebecca safe; beyond expectations, he had even managed to find Quinn and Corcoran, and learn something of what had happened to his friends. This evening, he wasn't certain if any of it made any difference. All that he had witnessed – the stunned townspeople, the faces of the injured, the ruined ground – swam before him as a kaleidoscope of images; but no solace, no answers. *What answer did you expect...?* He leaned on Tobey's withers and tried to clear his head.

"You alright?" Rebecca had appeared from the blue dusk and stood framed in the doorway.

Spencer picked his head up, "Yes. Just tired."

"I guess you'll be headed home tomorrow," she said, "I'm quite sure my sister is worried about you – and I don't want to be the cause of any more concern."

He looked to her and nodded, "I planned to leave first light tomorrow." He turned back and gazed into the small flame that worried at the side of the lantern glass. "But, I don't know; I feel there's something else..."

"Daniel," she said, "There's nothing more you need to do here. If you're staying here out of concern for me, thank you. As I said, I'll be fine now – thanks to you. But I don't think that's it."

She moved beside him and said softly. "Somehow I think it's easier for you to stay here than to go home. You said it yourself: you fit better in this nightmare. Do you think you don't deserve to be home?"

Spencer looked at her sharply, then back to the lantern. "Rebecca..." He knew she was right. "I don't know any more." He blew a long sigh and turned to her, "I'm just too tired to think on it now. And I think it's best I bed down out here..."

Rebecca smiled and raised her brow. "Well, there's one thing we do know: we don't need things any more difficult." She clasped his hand between hers.

"I think the answers you need now are at home. Things will look better in the morning, Daniel. Get some sleep. I know you'll be leaving early, but don't you go without saying goodbye." She squeezed his hand and returned to the house.

Daniel patted Tobey's flank, then stretched. He unrolled his blankets and spread them out on the hay. He sat, slowly pulled off his boots, and lay back, again trying to put the day in some sort of perspective. The whirl of images began anew and cut through his exhaustion. Over the ringing in his ears, he heard Rebecca's words clearly: *Do you think you don't deserve to be home...?*

He sat up abruptly and stared into the darkness. Despite all he had resolved for himself, one feeling still lingered: guilt, remorse that he had suffered less, that he could have done more. When others gave all, why was he still alive?

What would you do..? Would you lay there wounded..? Would you die instead of Quinn..?

Amidst the clamor of questions, he heard an answer, quiet at first – hesitant, but then louder. He spoke the words aloud.

"No," he said, "I chose to live…"

He heard Quinn's words from so long before: "*There's no winners...just survivors.*" The clamor stopped. Despite all he had learned, he had not *understood.*

"The only thing I did wrong was survive..."

Part of his burden was set aside. His thoughts quieted, the guilt faded to a whisper; in its place, sorrow for all that had passed – perhaps he could live with that. It was somewhere to start. The words rose again and faded, "*You need to get on with the rest of your life.*" He lay back, closed his eyes and fell fast asleep.

Daniel awakened again in the dark predawn, the last image of a dream before him. He passed through a vision illuminated in shimmering light; he walked with a smiling young woman and little girl, their faces were so brilliant as to be indistinct, but he knew in his heart that it was Sarah and their lost child. He recalled what Anna had said to him once: *Dreams are a gift from above, a vision of the future...* Since his return, the hellish images of his past had blotted out any chimera of a future. *A gift?* This cruel dream was no gift, he thought, just a glimpse of a lost future. But he knew what the vision meant: *We did not grieve; not together. We not only lost a child; we lost each other...* He rolled onto his side and gazed into the yard, warm tears blurring the waning moonlight.

July 9, 1863: Morning
Gettysburg

The deep orange rays of sunrise pressed at the back of Daniel's shirt, promising a scorching day to follow. *It's time to go...* Before dawn, he had Tobey saddled and was ready to leave. At the back of the Myers home, the kitchen once again bustled with activity. Daniel ducked in, thanking Sallie and her family for their help, and turned to step outside; Rebecca stood in the doorway.

"Can't get away that easy." She reached into her apron and pressed some envelopes into his hand. "I wrote some things for my family; please give everyone my love." She smiled, "I won't keep you, Daniel, but I wanted you to know how much I appreciated your coming. It was such a great help for these boys... And for me; having you here was what I needed." Rebecca held him tightly, then looked up at him. "But I hope you found some of what you were looking for as well."

"Thanks, Becky," he whispered, "Thanks for all you've done. As far as me...I still have some things to sort out, but I'm glad I came. Thanks. Be safe."

They embraced once more and Rebecca disappeared into the kitchen. Daniel pushed the letters Rebecca had given him for Sarah and her parents into his saddlebags. He mounted and made his way toward the edge of town deep in thought. *I hope you found some of what you were looking for...* Her words were still in his ears when he reached the Sheads' home by the Seminary. Beside the house, Jim Corcoran was busily pumping water from the well spigot with his good arm. Daniel rode across the yard and dismounted.

"Keeping you busy, are they? How you making out, Jim?"

"Well there you are," Corcoran said, "Doing pretty good all considered. Better than this damn well; you'd think there'd be more to pump after all that rain. Anyways, I figured it would take a while for you to get back. Had your hands full, haven't you? How's Quinn?"

"Well, Jim," he said quietly, "Quinn is gone."

Daniel tethered Tobey to the fence, sat beside the well and described the previous day as simply as he could; Corcoran kept pumping at the spigot, listening with a resigned look.

"I'm sorry, Spence," he said, "Damn shame. Quinn was a good man. When the time is right, I'll pass the news on to the other boys."

With two buckets filled, they returned to the Sheads' house, and passed out tins of the cool water among the wounded. Daniel took leave of those he knew, then walked outside and sat on the porch steps. He closed his eyes. The faces in the close rooms behind him became as one: young faces not so long ago, now the same sunken eyes and haunted countenance. Not so young anymore, Daniel noted, and certainly a different visage than their families at home awaited. How many would survive, he wondered, return home to pick up what remained of their lives? He shook his head and gazed across the wide slope toward the Seminary; the thought came again: *I survived...*

"Still thinking you should have been with the regiment?" Corcoran stood behind him. "I told you, Spence, there's nothing you could have done..."

"You know," Daniel shook his head, "Quinn said the same thing. No, I was just thinking about the long road ahead of those boys."

They walked to the side of the house where he had left Tobey to graze. It was time to go, but there was one thing more to do. Daniel studied the ridge behind the house; there were still things unanswered. He turned to Corcoran.

"It's time I get going, but I think I will take a look at the ground up there where the boys fought." He offered his hand to the lieutenant.

"Take care of yourself, Jim. If you or the boys need anything, you can go to the Myers home by the church; they can help."

"Don't you worry on it, Spence'," Corcoran smiled, "As I said, the Sheads folks are doing well by us; we'll get along fine. You just get back home and get settled. When I get out, I'll be stopping by and expecting a home-cooked meal." The lieutenant watched as Spencer untied Tobey and rode out across the yard; he blew a long sigh, and then limped back into the house.

Daniel passed through the torn orchard that covered the slope north of the Sheads home, and emerged on the crest just past the woods. There a farm wall paralleled the ridge; here, as on the hill south of town, it was plain the ground there had seen a bitter fight, for beyond the wall was a trampled field of grain, and rows of graves.

Closer to the wall, stood several individual burials marked with wooden slats. Daniel dismounted and read the nearest: *S. Gray, D, 16 Maine; Pvt. Wm. B., Co. E, 16th Mne.* The Maine regiment had been part of his old brigade. Just up the wall were three more graves; only one was marked: *G. Ruppry, B CO, 107 Penna.*

They didn't even get his name right... "Gid Ruppert," Spencer said aloud. He studied the trodden ground around him, and whispered to himself: "This is where they were…"

He studied the ridgeline, then turned back toward the flattened crops and freshly rowed graves in the valley behind. Corcoran had said the Rebs had hit them from three sides; the ground confirmed it. Spencer shook his head.

"Hell, they never had a chance…"

He could hear Quinn's voice on the breeze: *"Nothin' you could do would change what happened that day…"*

Daniel looked back over the wall at the ruined fields to the west. Still, there was no answer here. The battle was long since finished: the dead were gone, replaced by less grisly, anonymous piles of earth; in time, these too would disappear; the shattered fences will be mended, the torn fields plowed, and crops will sprout again. He recalled the torn hilltop where Quinn was buried. The thought arose again: *The ground will not scar forever, it doesn't remember...*

Daniel closed his eyes: the first man he had killed fell again before him, then the last; his comrades lay dead and dying around him too; then the faces of the survivors: the wounded, their desperate families, the stunned townspeople. If so many lives were changed forever, shouldn't something remain, some sign of all that had passed? How would anyone ever understand? *There's no forgetting...*

He heard the voice of the old man on the porch answer, "They's different kinds of hell."

Daniel gathered Tobey's reins and gazed over the torn ground. *It was my fate to survive, it is my obligation to remember.*

And I will never forget…

Across the valley, South Mountain rose to the west, its wooded slopes blue-green in the morning light. It was past time that he go. Sarah. *Blue eyes in the dawn…* There was so much that had long been unsaid. He gathered the reins, mounted, and rode across the scarred fields to the Chambersburg Road, riding west into the afternoon. Below the Cashtown Pass where he had watched Lee's wagons struggle, Daniel turned south down the valley toward his farm. At the foot of the mountain, he stopped briefly at the Spencer Mill, and spoke with his foreman and an apprentice. They had already returned and had the mill wheel in operation; there would be much to repair in the valley.

At last, Daniel reined Tobey up the slope to Jack Road. Now on a familiar path, the horse picked up his gait through the cool shade of the trees that lined the road. Halfway up the mountain, Daniel turned off and paused at the run. As when he passed just days before, the stream still ran broad and swift. He had grown accustomed to taking shallow breaths of foul atmosphere; now as he breathed deep of the cool wet air, the thought came again. *You survived.*

Just up the road, the Spencer lane began its narrow turn across the hillside. He rode slowly, and stopped at the curve where the ancient oak stood, studying the Rebel major's grave. It had been four days since they had buried the Southerner: it seemed like an age. He saw the man's face, imagined his family waiting in vain for his return. He reined Tobey up the road, and more images came: Rebecca, Sallie Myers, the pale woman in the green dress, the boy Elliot. One way or another, the war had changed all of them. *And me…*

He passed the barn and their stone house came into view. *"Doesn't seem like the same home you left, because you're not the same man who left..."* After all that had happened, he thought, at least this place was untouched; it was up to him how he would live with his memories.

Daniel dismounted and tied Tobey to the handrail at the porch. He patted the animal's flank and started up the broad steps. Above, the front door opened and Sarah stepped out, slowly at first, unsure, but then ran down the steps and held him.

"It's okay, Sarah. Rebecca is safe." he said.

Sarah looked up at him, her eyes that deep blue, with another question she was afraid to ask. He answered first.

"I'm home."

AFTERWORD

The auction of a family estate is a poignant affair: once treasured heirlooms lose their power to evoke memories of family and cherished times past, instead finding new value in the hands of strangers, mindless of the emotions the items once stirred. At one such auction, atop a cardboard box smelling vaguely of mildew, the auctioneer's sheet reads:

ESTATE AUCTION 9/28/09
SARAH WAGAMAN SPENCER ESTATE
Contents Box 8: Miscellaneous newspapers & files

Inside, amid the clippings from old newspapers, lies a folder containing a sheaf of dog-eared pages. On inspection, the documents appear in good shape for their apparent age, although several pages appear to be missing. The top sheet is typewritten, and numbered "Pg. 2" – perhaps an appropriate starting place, because it is apparent that you've walked into the middle of someone's life:

Military Pension Record of Daniel John Spencer
Cert. No. 567,469 / Widow's cert. no. 353,563

Mustered 7/25/1862 at Harrisburg, Penna.,
Commissioned Lieut., B Co., 107th Penna. Volunteer Infantry,
Commissioned Capt., B Co., 107th Penna. Volunteer Infantry, to date from 12/13/1862,
Resigned commission / Medical discharge due to exposure, date discharged for disability 2/20/63B. abt. 1836 at Chambersburg, Penna.

D. Aug 28, 1900 at Cashtown, Adams Co, Penna.

Married: April 21, 1861 at Gettysburg, Adams Co., Penna., by Rev. Abraham Essick

Spouse: Sarah Annabeth Wagaman b. Oct. 9, 1842 at Buchanan Valley, Adams Co., Penna

Children:

Daniel Conall Spencer: b. March 3, 1864 Cashtown, Adams Co, Penna.

Martha Ann Spencer: b. April 3, 1865 Cashtown, Adams Co, Penna.

Summary of Affidavits, etc. in Support of Pension Claims:

Jul 5, 1882 – Daniel J. Spencer, aged 46 years, resident of Adams Co, Penna.; claimed pension as result of poor health and debilitating pain due to wounds received during battle near Sharpsburg, Maryland, September 17, 1862, and at Fredericksburg, Virginia, December 13, 1862.

Discharged due to exposure February 20, 1863; reports that since leaving the service, he has resided at Adams Co, Penna., and his occupation is miller.

(continued)

The rest of the typed document appears to be missing, but in the bottom of the box is one more folder. The pages are foxed, blue-lined foolscap that show many creases and folds; unlike the previous pages, the writing is in the tight script of the nineteenth century.

Comments in Dedication to 107th Penna. Regiment Monument

Gettysburg, Penna.

September 11, 1889

I thank Brigadier General McCoy for his kind introduction and this opportunity to address you, my comrades. As most of you know, I had left the service by the time the regiment fought here at Gettysburg. However, as I live in sight of this famous field, I felt it my duty to offer my services to the Monuments Commission and the Commonwealth to make sure this marker came to completion.

I need not remind you the monument we dedicate here today is merely a page in the regiment's history; and no tablet of granite and bronze could add more honor to the deeds of the men who fell here. Yet this monument will serve to tell future generations of the deeds of those fought here and our comrades who offered their lives up in defense of their country.

As you can see, the eastern face of the stone reads: "107th Pennsylvania Regiment"; below, the text describes the actions of the regiment here at Gettysburg. The northern face speaks of the regiment's strength and losses here at Gettysburg. The southern face tells of the origins of the 107th and our service in the war. Fitting as it is, it doesn't seem to say enough, does it? Too many of our comrades lie in unmarked graves; too many returned home with their bodies stricken by wounds. Such is one cost of war.

That said, you can see that the monument's western face is blank. Here I have a notion for you to consider. Perhaps that face represents an untold cost of war: the story of those who survive. The warrior returns to his hearth and home, and begins to pick up the pieces of his life. Outwardly scarred or not, war leaves a mark on all those touched by its fire, a scar not so obvious as the others, but one that lingers on deep in the soul. As one of our comrades said to me after this battle: "There are no unwounded here." Like comrades with more visible wounds, not all suffer the same. But seldom does a day pass that all aren't reminded of what they endured, and how their lives have changed forever.

There is no moral here; no judgment of right or wrong. But if we must go to war to kill or be killed, which it seems we must, then we should be aware of this outcome as well. For some men, there are worse things in

war than death: surviving when comrades – perhaps more worthy – did not.

Perhaps in coming generations, people will finally speak of this other cost of war; perhaps they will not. Perhaps the doctors will wag their fingers, and say they understand this unseen wound; perhaps they will not. But for all we shared as comrades in arms, I think we share yet another bond in peace; that after one offers up one part of his life in service to his country, he offers up the rest of his life in service to that memory: in hopes that no one will not have to suffer such a war again.

The figures of the past go cloaked.
They walk in mist and rain and snow
And go, go slowly,
But they go.

- Wallace Stevens

Images

Note: Contemporary images accompanying the text were selected to compliment the storyline; some images portray a similar event.

"Invasion of Maryland - Crossing the Antietam" (NA) 13

"Soldiers at Rest" (NA) 15

South Mountain Above Gettysburg, From 1857 County Map 20

"Retreat From Gettysburg" (B&L) 21

Confederate Officer (Image based on original photograph) (LC) 28

"To Arms!" (HW) 30

"Maryland Battery at Antietam" (HW) 36

"Battle of Antietam" (Painting by B.T. Thurstrup) (LC) 37

"Antietam: Confederate dead in a Ditch on the Right Wing"

(Image based on original photograph) (LC) 46

"Civil War Surgeon" (HW) 50

"Dead Confederate Soldier, Petersburg, VA"

(Image from original photograph) (LC) 54

"Battery Going Into Position" (HW) 63

"Battle of Fredericksburg" (HW) 68

"Home Again" (Original painting by Trevor McClurg) (LC) 81

"Fredericksburg, Virginia" (NA) 84

"View of Hospital Tent" (HW) 86

"Fruitless Attempt to Cross the Rappahannock" (HW) 90

Gettysburg Area, From 1883 Bachelder Map of Gettysburg 113

"Union Dead Near McPherson's Woods" (B&L) 115

"Gettysburg, 1863" (NA) 117

"Trinity Episcopal Church, Unfinished Capitol In the

Background" (LC) 138

"Frederick, Maryland" (HW) 140

Frederick County, From 1858 map 142

"Fauquier Sulphur Springs Hotel, VA" (LC)   145

Emmitsburg Road, Maryland (HW)   149

"Headquarters, U.S. Sanitary Commission" (LC)   162

"View of Gettysburg" (NA)   181

"Gettysburg, Gateway of Cemetery" (LC)   183

"Lutheran Theological Seminary"(Image based on

    original photograph) (LC)   190

107th Pennsylvania Monument (PAG)   197

Unless otherwise noted, images are courtesy of:

John Archer lives in Gettysburg, Pennsylvania, where he is an historian and Licensed Battlefield Guide. HIs other written work includes: "East Cemetery Hill at Gettysburg," "Culp's Hill at Gettysburg," and "Fury On The Bliss Farm". The author's first work of historical fiction, "After the Rain," received Director's Mention for the Langum Prize in American Historical Fiction.

66353339R00115

Made in the USA
Middletown, DE
06 September 2019